GOODNIGHT TOKYO

Atsuhiro Yoshida

GOODNIGHT TOKYO

*Translated from the Japanese
by Haydn Trowell*

Europa
editions

Europa Editions
27 Union Square West, Suite 302
New York NY 10003
www.europaeditions.com
info@europaeditions.com

Copyright © YOSHIDA Atsuhiro, 2019
English translation rights arranged with Kadokawa Haruki Corporation,
through le Bureau des Copyrights Français, Tokyo.
First publication 2024 by Europa Editions

Translation by Haydn Trowell
Original title: *Oyasumi, Tokyo*
Translation copyright 2024 by Europa Editions

Library of Congress Cataloging in Publication Data is available
ISBN 979-8-88966-027-9

Yoshida, Atsuhiro
Goodnight Tokyo

Cover illustration by Massimo Dall'Oglio

Cover design by Ginevra Rapisardi

Prepress by Grafica Punto Print – Rome

Printed in Canada

CONTENTS

THE LOQUAT THIEF

The clock struck 1:00 A.M.

It must have been wound a little faster than the others, as the timepiece that Mitsuki was carrying sounded ahead of the countless others kept in the warehouse.

A few moments later a deluge of tones, some low and heavy, some dry and clear, competed to announce the coming of the hour.

The warehouse, easily large enough to hold two small airplanes, was filled with near endless rows of shelves and drawers, its walls lined with clocks and paintings and calendars and tapestries and the like until there was little room for anything else.

Those shelves and drawers were filled with all sorts of knick-knacks, items of every size and shape imaginable that told the story of everyday lives in Japan for the past three hundred years.

You could find practically anything in here.

For example, if one of the directors told her that he wanted a travel trunk from the Taisho era, all she had to do was find it within the limits of this building and promptly deliver it to the set prior to shooting.

Mitsuki was what was known as a *procurer*, and she had been working at this large film company on the outskirts of Tokyo for almost five years.

The wall clock that she was presently carrying was for a 9:00 A.M. shoot. There were several other items that she had to prepare as well, most of which could be found inside the warehouse. The timepiece that she had unearthed was a perfect fit for the director's requirement for something *classical and with gravitas*. Carrying it carefully with both hands, she traced her steps back to the assistant director in the waiting room. While everyone called it a waiting room, it was simply a small area to store props that the film crew intended to use in an upcoming shoot, not a place for actors to wait before entering the set.

Mitsuki would have preferred to work on large-scale stage sets. She had always longed for a job where she could make life-size sets that looked exactly like the real thing, to actually *create* an entire corner of a fictional town. But the very moment she set foot into the prop warehouse on her first day of training, she had fallen instantly in love.

The warehouse was a gigantic box crammed with every kind of object one might think of, and Mitsuki had been fascinated by small miscellaneous *things* ever since she was a young girl.

She remembered being particularly obsessed with old medicine chests, their lids opening to reveal bags and bottles printed with all sorts of colorful symbols and small lettering. Bandages, antiseptics, eye drops, plasters, ointments—to a child's eye, each one had looked special.

That same fascination blossomed in her heart all over again upon discovering the warehouse, to the point that she felt like letting out an excited squeal. The past itself was preserved amid the miscellany of objects here. For Mitsuki, the prop warehouse was nothing short of a time capsule encompassing a full three hundred years, and each time she stepped inside she was overcome with elation, as if setting out on a new little adventure. Then came the added fun of seeking out the best items to meet the directors' requests—tasks that she relished as though engrossed in a child's game.

The only problem was that Mitsuki herself wasn't compatible with time. Or, strictly speaking, she always found herself out of step with clocks, like the one she was currently holding in her arms.

Clocks were her natural enemy, and the reason for that was simple enough. Her internal body clock and the laidback personality that it had imparted her with were constantly at odds with the endlessly harrying—as she saw it—clocks of the modern world. And so she often found herself bristling at the deadlines that the directors gave her.

With a dull tone, one more clock, somewhere deep in the warehouse, struck 1:00 A.M.

It was probably the slowest one in the whole collection.

That one's me, isn't it? The slowest clock of them all.

With a deep breath, she tightened her grip on the antique timepiece cradled in her arms.

"See you tomorrow," Mitsuki said after handing the wall clock to the assistant director, Mizushima.

She was about to call it a day when Mizushima held her back. "Actually, there's one more thing."

"This is everything on the list you gave me, though?"

"There's a new addition. And we'll need 'em by nine o'clock. A bunch of fresh loquats."

"Loquats?"

"Yeah, loquats. The fruit. Not kumquats. Loquats."

"I know what you meant . . . "

So she said, but in truth, Mitsuki had never purchased a loquat before. At the very least, she had never had to procure one for work, and she didn't recall ever having bought one personally from a greengrocer or a supermarket.

She *had* eaten one once, she remembered that, but the specifics—where exactly she had eaten it, what it tasted like—eluded her.

That was one of the consequences of working at a job like hers—always having to look back on her life so far, to reflect on the experiences its journey had given her and those it hadn't.

Pressure cookers, for example. Silk hats. Unicycles.

More often than not, she was completely ignorant about the items that one director or another expected her to provide. She had lived a full twenty-seven years, and still she understood nothing whatsoever about them.

It was the same for loquats. She didn't know whether they were even available in early summer.

"I did look into it a bit myself," Mizushima said, as if reading her thoughts. "This is just based on what I read online, but they're still in season, just barely. There has to be somewhere that still has them this time of year."

"Oh, I see." The next moment, Mitsuki's voice picked up. "But in Tokyo?"

Mizushima flashed her a forced grin. When he smiled like that, it inevitably meant that the road ahead was going to be a bumpy one. In short, his expression just now anticipated difficulties in sourcing loquats.

"Besides, think about the time," Mitsuki added, her shoulders slumping.

"Right, yeah. There won't be a whole lot of greengrocers open at this hour. I'd suggest having a look in the all-night supermarkets, but there seem to be fewer and fewer of them around these days."

Mitsuki responded with a silent nod. When society and the economy were booming, all-night shops popped up all over the place. And just as Mizushima had said, their numbers had fallen dramatically in recent years.

"Yep," the assistant director whispered, as though his words were meant not for Mitsuki, but for himself. "Nights in Tokyo are starting to feel awful lonely lately."

Matsui sipped at his can of coffee in the office's half-lit break room while waiting for his shift to start.

The cab company where he worked was called Blackbird, specializing in serving customers from evening through to early morning. The cars were dark blue in tint, almost black, and the drivers wore similarly colored uniforms. Being a small company, Blackbird only had a limited fleet of vehicles, with most of its business coming from advance bookings. Recently, however, the number of such customers had been on a steady decline, forcing the fleet to turn to picking up customers on the street. And so tonight, Matsui found himself stuffing the blank reservation list into his pocket when he let out a sudden sneeze.

Maybe someone was badmouthing him around town? But even if so, it wasn't like there was anything he could do about it.

Yes, if someone *was* criticizing him behind his back this late at night, it could only be a customer. He couldn't think of anyone else who would bother to go to all that effort. He had hit his fifties while still a bachelor, he had been born and raised in Tokyo, which meant that he had no other hometown he might return to, and being an only child whose parents had died young, he had spent a lifetime away from anything even resembling family.

He was, he remarked to himself, a boring man.

When asked by a colleague why he had become a taxi driver, he could answer only that he had just sort of wound up in the role.

But there was at least one small twist of fate that had guided him down this path.

As a child, he had stumbled upon a picture book titled *The Car is the Color of the Sky* at the local library. The main character was a taxi driver called Mr. Matsui, who sometimes picked up strange passengers like bears and foxes. He remembered positively devouring the book, all the while imagining how fun it would be to have such a job.

Whenever he closed the cover after reading the book, he would stare at the picture of Mr. Matsui in his light blue cab.

This, he thought to himself, was what he would one day become.

And so he did. Over the past thirty years, he had moved from one company to the next, each time changing the color of his vehicle.

But he still hadn't come across a sky-blue taxi.

After leaving the break room, he made his way to the garage and his parked car—not a bright blue, but a deep one, almost black. The garage was roofless, exposed to the wind, and when he looked up he could take in the sky and a yellow banana-shaped moon. The stars were barely visible. The usual dreary Tokyo night scene.

Hmm? At that moment, his gaze passing between his vehicle and the night sky, he suddenly realized something.

"So they *are* the same color, huh?" he mumbled.

Then, all of a sudden, his cellphone began to ring.

He quickly pulled the device from his pocket and glanced down at the screen.

Beneath the cold anonymity of the eleven-digit number was a name: Mitsuki Sawatari.

Looks like Matsui is my only choice, Mitsuki thought with a sigh.

She felt bad having to call on him again like this. How many times now had she turned to him for help, unable to find what she needed for herself?

She hastened to lower the phone and end the call, when her eyes fell on faint glimmer reflecting from her left ring finger.

"Oh . . . " sounded her voice weakly.

The ring had been a gift from Koichi.

Just three days ago, she had finally been able to meet her boyfriend Koichi on her first day off in longer than she could remember.

"I'm sorry," she had said. "I didn't have any free time this week." "I've been so busy." "Sorry again." "Next week, I promise."

For the past month, every time he called asking to meet, she had ended up turning him down. It was true that things had been hectic at the studio, but there was another reason for these constant postponements.

Why? Because Koichi had asked for her ring size. Her ring finger, he had specified—though he had never once mentioned the word *engagement*.

But he was always like that. Mitsuki could hardly stand it.

Koichi was three years her junior, and she would have liked to say she didn't feel the age gap—but in fact, the opposite was true. He had a natural little brother personality, and he was constantly demanding her attention or else begging for her help. Once, he had even told her upfront: "I want you to take care of me in life."

"What's the problem?" Aiko, a close friend of hers had asked her. "He sounds adorable."

But perhaps because she had lost her father at a young age, Mitsuki would have sooner had a partner willing to indulge *her*, not the other way around.

"Then why don't you break up with him?"

Given what Mitsuki wanted for herself, Aiko's suggestion was no doubt the right one. Yet Mitsuki was touched by Koichi's dedication and single-mindedness—even if that devotion wasn't meant for her.

"One of the crows," Koichi began all of a sudden during their rendezvous.

He arrived at the restaurant on the top floor of a hotel in Shinjuku ten minutes late. Throughout all their years together, they had never been to a place like this before, making it a rare extravagance for the both of them. With the expansive night view outside the window, it felt like they were dining beyond the limits of the sky.

"One of the crows, it made a bookshelf."

Mitsuki was unable to make heads or tails of this bizarre

statement—but playing the role of a wise older sister, she did her best to coax out what he wanted to say.

"A bookshelf?" she repeated.

"The old crow was collecting books, you see."

"Oh? Where?"

"On its bookshelf. It brought a piece of plywood or something to the top of an oak tree and built a shelf there. I was observing it the whole time. It started arranging all these books and magazines that it must have taken from people's garbage. Seriously, it was one smart little guy."

Koichi was a subcontractor brought into the Crow Control Initiative set up by the Tokyo Metropolitan Government Environment Bureau. Or rather, that was his self-proclaimed role. His real job was delivering newspapers. Making his rounds during the early hours of the morning, he had developed a pronounced curiosity for crows, and before long, he took to observing their ecology. While he had no qualifications to his name, the experience and knowledge gleaned from his many years of observation had been well-received by professional scholars, with some even turning to him for his insights and opinions.

There was a park with a large grove near his apartment, a place that served as a roosting area for crows. A train line ran next to the park, and one day the editor of a free newsletter distributed at the station reached out wanting to interview Koichi. Thanks to that article, Koichi earned a reputation as the city's resident Crow Professor. Mitsuki had been a student back then, working part time as the editor's assistant, and as such, she had accompanied him during the interview. She later pulled an all-nighter to write the clumsy article detailing the Crow Professor's many observations.

That was how she first met Koichi. And so the two of them had been dating for a good many years.

However, as far as she was concerned, their relationship had barely changed since their student days. Koichi may have gone to the trouble of dressing up in a fancy suit and booking a table at a restaurant in a luxury hotel, but he had completely forgotten the purpose of the dinner, going on and on and on about a crow building a bookshelf. It was no different to that rambling, incoherent interview.

"Hey, you know . . . " Mitsuki interrupted, stopping him once the meal was over and the waiter brought out dessert. "Didn't you have something you wanted to say to me?

There had been no real forewarning as such, but after being asked her ring size and with Koichi inviting her to an expensive restaurant, there could only be one possible explanation.

"Ah, right." He rummaged through the inner pocket of his jacket, presenting her with a red box tied with a white ribbon. "I almost forgot."

That was all.

Mitsuki knew perfectly well what it was, but having lost all patience with him, she asked bluntly: "What is it?"

She proceeded to tear off the ribbon, opening the lid as if it was no more than a box of caramels. "What's this?" she asked again, yanking the ring out and jamming it on her left ring finger. Then, as if only joking, she tried to pull it off.

The ring, however, wouldn't budge.

Huh? Tilting her head in an effort to keep Koichi from noticing, she applied even more force—but no, it was firmly stuck.

She had meant to remove it right away, and even had her next words already planned out. "I can't accept this unless you explain to me exactly what it is."

But if it wouldn't come off, she could hardly say anything like that.

Try as she might to remove it, the ring was fixed in place, clinging to her finger like a thing alive.

Mitsuki was standing next to a supermarket's neon sign, lips curled in a pout, when Matsui arrived to pick her up. The taxi's *Reserved* sign stood out brightly in the murky dark.

"I'm screwed," she murmured as she stepped into the vehicle.

"What happened?" Matsui asked, watching her in the rearview mirror.

"This is the sixth all-night supermarket I've been to. At least this time I got to talk to someone who actually knows what's what when it comes to stocking fruit, but when I asked him if he knew anywhere that would still be selling them, he said I'd be hard-pressed to find them *anywhere* in Tokyo . . . "

"Fruit, you said?"

Matsui was puzzled as to the problem, but this wasn't the first time that Mitsuki had called him to help in some bizarre collection task. In that sense, she was one of his few reliable repeat customers.

"Here I am turning to you again, Matsui. I'm sorry. I wanted to find them on my own this time, but I'm not having any luck."

"And what are you looking for today?"

"Loquats. The fruit. Not kumquats. Loquats . . . Right, speaking of fruits, didn't you help me run all over Tokyo looking for green apples once, even though they were out of season?"

"Yes, that was a real head-scratcher." Despite his words, Matsui sounded like he was looking back over a fond memory.

"But if even the store clerk thinks there aren't any to be found, where should I go?" Mitsuki asked.

Matsui started driving. "Well, where do you want to start?" He glanced at her through the rearview mirror.

Mitsuki's eyes were downcast, her eyebrows furrowed as she fidgeted with something on her left hand. "Oh, it just won't come off," she murmured with a sigh.

Matsui turned his attention back to the road. "If nowhere in Tokyo has any, maybe we should look outside of Tokyo?"

Leaving the city meant going either north or west. Matsui

turned onto one of the main roads and began drawing a mental map as he considered which way to go. The streets were empty tonight. A lone motorcycle overtook them, speeding comfortably past.

"Ah. Can you wait a minute?" Mitsuki took her hand away from the ring, checking the incoming message on her cellphone as she nodded her head. "Uh-huh."

"What is it?"

"Um, yes . . . " she paused for a moment to finish reading the message. "Is the main intersection at Sakuradani far from here?"

"No. It will probably take around fifteen minutes to get there."

"Around fifty meters from the intersection, on the road to Fukagawacho—it says here there's supposed to be a tree there. According to this, it had loquats on it yesterday."

"Oh? That's very precise information."

Matsui sounded surprised, but he couldn't have been any more amazed than Mitsuki herself. A few minutes earlier, she had sent Koichi a text message asking if he might know anywhere that she could find loquats. She hadn't really expected to receive a reply.

You were awake? she hurriedly texted him back.

About to head out on deliveries, came his response.

How did you know about the loquat tree?

Crows like to take the fruits once they've ripened.

Ah. Mitsuki was impressed. His knowledge could actually prove useful at times.

Koichi took little interest in anything other than crows. If you were to ask him what interesting experiences life had brought him, his responses would be about nothing else.

He had lived without worrying about pressure cookers, or silk hats, or unicycles. Mitsuki suspected that he had never so much as tasted a loquat.

But perhaps he was a living example that if you master one specific thing, it can lead you to so many others. Even if he didn't know the first thing about loquats, crows, it seemed, had nonetheless led him to them.

"Uh-huh," Mitsuki nodded to herself in realization as the vehicle approached Sakuradani.

"We're almost there."

Startled by Matsui's voice, she pressed her face up against the window to check the roadside trees one by one.

Only then did she realize that she had no idea what a loquat tree even looked like. And it was the middle of the night. The streetlamps provided some illumination, so maybe she could try identifying the fruits from their color? But it would probably be better to step outside and investigate on foot.

"I'll wait here, then," Matsui said, pulling over on the side of the road.

Mitsuki stepped outside and started walking, scrutinizing the trees.

But she couldn't spot what she needed.

She began to doubt whether her memories of loquats—their size, their color—were truly accurate.

If she wasn't mistaken, they were meant to be light orange.

The ones sold in stores were definitely that color, but maybe they were a different hue while still on the tree? Perhaps they were greener, the color of young grass, only ripening after they had fallen from the branch?

It was certainly possible. And so she set about peering into the trees once more.

At that moment, a flash of orange entered the corner of her vision.

"That's it!" she exclaimed—when the fruit was obscured behind a dark mass. Whatever it was, she couldn't help but feel like the *thing* had snatched the loquat away.

A crow? Mitsuki braced herself.

It *had* to be a crow. There was no question about it. Clinging to the branch, an unbelievably huge crow was grabbing the orange fruits one after another.

No, wait a minute.

Just as Mitsuki told herself that there couldn't possibly be a crow that large, a truck passed by, its headlights illuminating the tree and revealing the identity of the shadowy creature.

It was a person.

Black hair and a black jacket. Not a man, but a woman.

"Um," Mitsuki called out cautiously.

For a brief moment, a chill ran down her spine—but as her eyes adjusted to the darkness, she could clearly make out a tall, slender woman scrambling further up the tree.

"Um, excuse me? What are you doing up there?"

The woman startled for a moment, but maybe this wasn't the first time that someone had caught her in the act. She stared down at Mitsuki and answered without hesitation: "I'm a loquat thief."

"It's just around the corner. Why don't you stop by?"

Hidden inside the woman's black jacket were magnificent loquats, exactly as Mitsuki had imagined. Naturally, she remained on her guard, but she couldn't turn her back on this chance. So long as she had Matsui with her, she reasoned, she would be fine—and so she accepted the invitation to drop by the apartment of this self-proclaimed loquat thief.

"Please," the woman said, and with no more warning than that, pulled out three glasses and poured them all a cup of golden loquat wine.

"Last year's batch," the loquat thief said in a mellow voice.

Every year, she would climb loquat trees in the middle of the night, harvest the fruits, and turn them into liqueur.

"My brother used to do this all the time," she explained.

She looked over at a frame on the corner of the cupboard—a

photo of a smiling man, much younger than the woman but almost identical in appearance.

The woman looked back to Mitsuki with a faint smile. "But you're telling me this bunch will make its way onto the big screen?"

Just one bunch would do, Mitsuki had insisted.

"Alright," the woman answered readily enough. She seemed amused by Mitsuki's job title of *procurer*. "They'll be the stars of the show, right? They're already stolen goods, so don't hold back. Take as many as you want. I might have a little less to make into next year's wine, but I'll be able to enjoy looking out for them in a big-name film, right?"

The woman had called herself a loquat thief, and she had indeed taken the fruit without anyone's permission. But putting aside that one small crime once a year, she was a remarkably earnest, even tireless, individual. She wore a white business shirt beneath her black jacket, and while her makeup was modest, her facial features were those of a traditional Japanese beauty—not that she was one to boast of her own good looks. No, she worked through the night day after day, hardly ever making use of her vacation time.

Tonight was a rare day off, allowing her to take on the mantle of the loquat thief, but she would normally spend these late-night hours in an operator's room, responding to the incessant barrage of phone calls as they came in.

"It's always some nameless person on the other end of the line. Young and old, men and women, they call in looking for someone to talk to about their problems, everything from silly life advice to serious life-and-death issues."

Mitsuki accepted this explanation without further question. After all, it was thanks to that friendly, dependable voice that she had let her guard down, even though she had never once met this woman before.

"I'm with the Tokyo No. 3 Consultation Room. If you need

anything, give me a call," the woman said, handing Mitsuki her business card. "I might be able to help with your *procurement*. And of course, I'm always happy to talk about love affairs or family problems or the like."

Mitsuki closed her eyes as she savored the complex taste of the loquat wine, its wonderful contrast of sweet and sour. Matsui was still on the job, so he merely tasted it with the tip of his tongue and relished its aroma.

"Hey, Matsui?" Mitsuki asked as she leaned deep into the back seat of the taxi, cradling a handful of loquats on her lap. "I think I'm going to nod off here."

The loquat wine was having an effect, a sugary drowsiness taking hold of her body.

"I understand. Please, go ahead. I'll take you back to your apartment."

"No, don't do that. If I go to bed, I'll never be able to wake up. Just keep driving around until dawn, please."

"Very well," Matsui answered, watching her through the rearview mirror.

Mitsuki, her eyes already closed, reached out to the ring glimmering on her left hand, gently stroking its surface with her fingertip as she dozed off. Her face was as innocent as an angel's.

For Tokyo too, it was time for the briefest moments of shuteye.

With the city asleep, wrapped in the warm embrace of night, only the loquat fruits stood out, softly reflecting the dim moonlight.

Lost at 4:00 a.m.

The clock showed exactly 1:00 A.M.

From this point on, it was rush hour at the Tokyo No. 3 Consultation Room.

Kanako Fuyuki had found just enough time to tidy up the items on her desk, pausing to catch her breath and take in the night sky outside the window.

Her company was on the fourth floor of a five-story building twelve minutes from the nearest train station.

This was where she worked—Desk 25 in the call center.

From 10:00 P.M. through to 7:00 A.M., she took calls for eight hours with an hour-long break in the middle. There were three separate shifts—morning, afternoon, and evening—and she was part of the evening group. At the beginning of each shift, the daytime operators would fill her in on the day's events.

"Good morning."

That night, she was taking over from a younger colleague, Shinichi Goto.

"We've had one small hiccup today," Goto began.

Sometimes, Kanako hated that unwavering smile of his—at others, she found it heartwarming.

"It's the voice bank phone. You know, that old model?" he asked her.

"Ah," Kanako answered vaguely.

The voice bank was mainly handled by the daytime staff, so the night crew wasn't particularly familiar with the system. It looked like a regular telephone, albeit an old-fashioned model.

Simply put, it was an automated answering machine. When the operators were busy, calls would be automatically redirected to the voice bank, which recorded callers' concerns. In rare cases, callers might leave their phone number, and when they did, one of the staff would call them back after listening to the recording.

However, the majority of calls to the Consultation Room were anonymous, with clients unwilling to share any identifying information. In many cases, they simply wanted someone to talk to. As such, when met with a recorded message, most simply hung up or else responded with some one-line sentence like *I'll call back later*.

"The decision has been made to dispense with it."

"*Dispense* with it?"

Kanako couldn't fail to miss Goto's old-fashioned turn of phrase. It was an occupational disease, of sorts. In this job, one could only get a real impression of the individual on the other end of the line through their use of language. In other words, those who had a wide vocabulary and strong abilities of articulation tended to make good operators.

"Yes," Goto answered, nonplussed. "I don't know why, but apparently, management is introducing some new system, and the answering machine is no longer necessary."

"I see," Kanako answered with a slight nod. "So what's the problem?"

"Someone at the disposal service is coming by to pick it up. At four in the morning."

"At that hour? Why?"

"It was their idea. We're open twenty-four seven, so basically, they know that any time will work for us. I don't know why, but it sounds like it's a bit of a headache to delete all the personal data on it. Anyway, they were pretty insistent."

"Uh-huh."

"Not *Uh-huh*, Kanako. I need you to hand it over to them when they come to pick it up."

"Ah, I see."

It was a trivial request, but it piqued her interest nonetheless. This too was an occupational disease, of sorts.

Why would someone want to pick up a discarded telephone at that time of day? Was it simply for the driver's personal convenience? Or was the disposal company another twenty-four-hour business, the kind of place with one of those mottos like *If there's something you want to get rid of, give us a call, any time, any day?*

But really, in the middle of the night?

"Interesting. *Very* interesting," she murmured under her breath as she glanced over the list of A-class calls that Goto had handed her.

Of all the calls received by the daytime shift, those deemed worth continuing were earmarked as A-class. Naturally, the evening staff likewise compiled their own list of A-class calls, to be passed on to the morning shift. There were a few brief notes, but the overwhelming majority of the entries were marked as *looking for someone to listen* rather than *serious consultation.*

While the company ostensibly offered consultation services, most callers didn't necessarily have any real problems or concerns. The majority simply wanted someone to talk to, someone to lend a friendly ear. For Kanako, belonging to the evening shift, it seemed only natural that people would seek out someone to chat with when facing the small hours awake and alone.

She had originally been a caller herself, as indeed had most of the other consultants.

"I understand. 4:00 A.M."

"The driver will be asking for you directly, so make sure you're not on a call. You'll close with that today."

"Huh?" Kanako peered into Goto's face. He was a smooth talker, but sometimes the words coming out of his mouth didn't make any sense.

"What do you mean *close*?" she repeated.

"Apparently, they want you to be present."

"Present? For what?"

"Like I said, to dispose of the phone. I don't really under-stand it myself, but that's just how it is."

"Hold on. How *what* is? You're saying they want me to watch them throw away a telephone?"

"It sounds like it. Because of all the voicemails and personal information stored in it, apparently."

Kanako fought the urge to raise her voice. "But couldn't they just smash it with a hammer or something?" she asked, gesturing with her hands.

"Well, I don't personally see why not." Goto paused, check-ing the memo that he had received from the team leader. "But it's written here loud and clear: *Disposing of old equipment is a solemn affair, practically a funeral. Please ensure that it is com-pletely destroyed and incinerated.*"

"Chief Mochida wrote that?"

"I don't know. It was probably them, the company that's going to dispose of it. I'm not sure." He shook his head, before handing her the piece of paper with *4:00 A.M.* scribbled in large letters. "Anyway, whatever the vendor wants, just go along with them."

"Uh-huh."

Kanako took the note in her hands, her eyes drawn to the words *destroyed and incinerated*, much smaller than the time *4:00 A.M.*

There could be no explaining it, but the operators in the call center sometimes spoke of a phenomenon by which certain words and phrases seemed to repeat in close proximity.

As had been the case tonight.

In the three hours between 11:00 P.M. and 2:00 A.M., Kanako had taken calls from twelve separate clients. Three of them, though of different ages, genders, and circumstances, each said more or less the same thing: *I can't find the last one.* Of course, they all had their own unique stories to tell.

"I want to move on to the next stage of my life, but I just need one last little push. You know, one final trigger. But I can't seem to find that last one."

"I'm collecting those Transformation Balls that come in packets of Fireman candy. But for some reason, I can't find the last one."

"The string on my necklace broke. Really, this is the worst. The beads went all over the place. There are supposed to be twenty-eight of them, but no matter where I look, I just can't find the last one."

The phrases *I can't find it* and *I'm looking for something* were standard in a consultant's line of work.

But what struck Kanako most were the words *the last one* strung on at the end. The combination with *I can't find it* sent little bubbles rising up from the depths of her memory.

Was this what he—her younger brother—had been searching for, at the very beginning?

I suppose my earliest memory is of the Hachiman Festival.

During her break at two o'clock, Kanako sipped at a can of coffee and stared out the window at the bleak trees lining the street.

I was in third grade at the time, so he would have been in first grade.

Her mother had instructed her to take her brother to the local shrine. It was their first time going alone, and they had been strictly warned to come home before sundown.

Her brother, however, was a free spirit, and he wasn't the kind to listen to what his parents had to say. His carefree attitude only served to double her worries, but she was unable to say that to him directly. She hated the way he acted, but at the same time, she found it somehow heartwarming.

On top of that, her brother was so much more independent than every other boy Kanako had ever known. He casually refused to participate in the same activities as other children—but rather than reject them outright, he would effortlessly separate himself from the group and pursue his own interests.

That was why he got lost so often. How many times had Kanako heard his name, Ren Fuyuki, announced over loudspeakers and PA systems at department stores and amusement parks?

"Good afternoon, ladies and gentlemen. There is a missing boy named—"

Right, it's been a while since I last heard those words.

With festival grounds being as busy as they were, they were practically asking for children to get separated from their parents. And so Kanako always held Ren's body snugly against her own.

But even so . . .

Realizing that Ren was no longer next to her, she startled. "Eh?" she exclaimed, but no matter where she looked, she couldn't find him.

"Oh," she mouthed in a show of despair, deciding to check the stalls one by one.

Even now, she would break into what others might call a *troubled face* at the slightest hint of something amiss. At times, there wasn't even anything to be worried about.

"Kanako? What's wrong?" people would ask.

Back then, however, she truly was frantic, running to and fro in search of her brother.

So many different smells and colors flooded her senses: the smell of yakisoba sauce, the vibrant orange of apricot candies, the emerald green and sweet aroma of melon soda, the fragrance of corn cobs on the grill, silver superhero masks, the dusty odor of a shooting range with a red velvet curtain.

Her brother was nowhere to be found.

"Where are you, Ren?" she called out.

That was when she spotted it—a stall. She could hardly believe her eyes. It was filled with transparent glass spheres, each around the size of the globe in her classroom at school.

They looked like they were floating in the air.

There must have been at least ten of them. At first glance, they didn't look like they were suspended by strings. And there were objects trapped inside each of them. Everything from miniature cars, to harmonicas, to chocolate bars, to small bouquets of flowers, even wristwatches. No matter where she looked, there was something encased within a glass sphere.

Around that small stall, gravity seemed to be non-existent. Colorful toys and sweets floated freely, and staring intently at them was her brother, as if possessed.

"Ren!" she cried at the top of her lungs.

She surprised herself with how loud she called out, but if she didn't, she knew that her brother would just run off somewhere else. Her mind was gripped by bizarre fantasies, like things she had read in books—he might end up trapped in one of those glass spheres floating in midair, or he might even be carried off to another world . . .

She called out again as she approached—and that was when it happened.

A man in a black hat standing at the end of the stall put his hand over his mouth, and all of a sudden, a transparent glass ball shot out from between his lips.

Kanako watched on, agape, unable to move, while her brother looked almost ecstatic. The sphere continued to swell, stretching, expanding.

"I think they used to sell that kind of thing at festivals and the like. You know what I mean?" Kanako once tried asking the woman who ran her favorite bar.

Though a voluptuous beauty, the woman on the other side of the counter had been born a man. She kept her age a secret, though she must have been similar enough to Kanako in years, as they had grown up around the same time in the same small corner of Tokyo.

"Ah, those!" The proprietress was always ready to answer Kanako's questions, no matter the topic. "Yeah, they had them in candy stores too, right? We used to call them toy balloons. I thought they were made from glue? They're not glass, anyway. Basically, it's like bubblegum. You put a chunk of smelly glue on the end of a straw and blow into it."

Kanako sometimes found it difficult to distinguish between memory and dream, and so she would often discuss her recollections with the woman to try to get to the truth. She was the only person Kanako could turn to for advice late at night, and at the same time, she was her only true friend in all of Tokyo.

"Woah," Ren exclaimed, trying to act older than his years, as the man inflated another sphere.

"I was standing next to him, gripping his hand while we watched the man. We were always like that . . . "

The woman peered into Kanako's *troubled face* with gentle eyes.

"But before I knew it, he was gone. I had let go." Kanako averted her gaze, her shoulders slumping.

"It wasn't your fault," the proprietress said, placing a large hand atop hers. "You can't hold onto someone forever. Especially not after they grow up."

"I know. But still . . . "

"How many years is it now?"

"Twelve."

"They pass so quickly."

"Sometimes. Sometimes, they take forever."

One day, Ren vanished from the apartment where they had been living together. Kanako would have liked to be able to say that he disappeared without warning, and yet—

I guess that *was his warning . . .*

Every now and then, that memory would flash again before her eyes.

"There doesn't seem to be anything for us to investigate right now."

Such had been the police officer's conclusion at the time of his disappearance.

"But my brother, he—"

"He might have decided to move out. Or maybe he lost his bearings on the way home."

Ren had been approaching his twenty-fourth birthday, so he wasn't a child anymore. The police officer must have been joking.

But Kanako knew, intuitively—he *did* get lost.

"I can't find the last one . . . "

That was what he had said that morning.

At the time, Kanako had just secured a job at a trading company with the help of a friend. She had resolved to support her brother, who instead of finding work himself, spent his days reading, supposedly to cultivate knowledge and wisdom.

"The last what?" she asked half-heartedly, about to leave for work. "What can't you find?"

"The last piece of the jigsaw puzzle."

"Jigsaw puzzle?"

She hadn't realized that he had taken an interest in such things. Maybe Ren had wanted to tell her more about the puzzle, but she was running late for her train. "I hope you find it," she said abruptly and dashed out of their apartment.

That was the last conversation she ever had with him.

"Hey," the bar woman said, her voice flooding out Kanako's reminiscence. "It's time to put it behind you. Forget about him."

Unsure how to respond, Kanako sat there in melancholy silence.

"I understand how you feel, you know? It's contagious, that

feeling like you need to find something. But it's not a puzzle, not exactly. It's more like a game."

"I see." Kanako's reply was half-hearted, just as it had been back then.

I've come this far without finding the last piece of the puzzle my brother was looking for . . .

It was probably such a trivial thing, that missing piece.

She didn't know what kind of puzzle he was trying to complete. He might have even meant it as a metaphor.

In the end, whether a physical puzzle or a product of the imagination, it was a picture that could only be completed by connecting one piece to the next.

But while it may have been on the cusp of completion, without the final piece, the one that Ren seemed to have misplaced, there could be no telling precisely what the picture really was.

"By the way, did you ever find it? That puzzle Ren was going on about?"

"No. Not yet."

"Not the last piece. The puzzle itself, I mean."

The answer's the same.

Even if by some stroke of luck she somehow managed to find the missing piece in the crannies of the carpet, she still probably wouldn't be able to figure out what the finished puzzle was supposed to look like.

Then again, maybe one day, just maybe, she *would* find it while tidying up.

Holding the nozzle of the vacuum cleaner in her right hand, she would reach down and retrieve the smallest of jigsaw puzzle pieces in mute shock—and in that moment, the image might finally come together.

"Thank you for waiting," said the worker from the disposal company.

Reflexively, Kanako glanced at her watch. It was three minutes past four.

To her surprise, it was a young woman who had come to pick up the telephone. Even more unexpectedly, she was as straight as a ruler, and was dressed in black mourning clothes.

"Um . . ."

Kanako found herself staring at the woman's outfit. It looked like it hadn't been ironed in quite some time.

"Should I have worn something like that?" she asked.

The woman glanced down at her clothes. "No, not at all," she replied with a quick shake of her head.

She seemed to have concluded just as quickly that Kanako was going to be a troublesome customer.

"If there are any problems, please reach out to us," the woman said as if by rote, handing her a business card. "Moriizumi. I know what you're thinking, but it's one name— it's *not* the surname Mori and given name Izumi." This too she seemed to have practiced many times before. Given how common those names were in Japan, that perhaps wasn't surprising.

"I see. Moriizumi," Kanako repeated, before offering her a copy of her own business card in turn.

Without even looking at the card, Moriizumi stuffed it into her blouse pocket. "Alright then. I'll dispose of it properly."

She picked up the cardboard box containing the telephone and tucked it under one arm with practiced ease. Then, as if by magic, she produced a slip of paper, indicating where Kanako was to sign.

Once Kanako had scribbled her name in the box, Moriizumi quickly shoved the slip into her pocket and turned to leave.

"Um, wait, please," Kanako called out. "I'll go with you."

"Huh?" Moriizumi broke into a slight frown, eyeing Kanoko curiously. "You want to come with me?"

"Er, I mean . . ." Kanako wasn't quite sure what to say. She hadn't expected that she would need to bring funeral attire. "I was told I'm supposed to be present during the disposal."

Moriizumi was already making her way back to the elevator, ignoring Kanako's nonsensical insistence.

This is the last one. I just want to finish early and go home. Then I can take a shower, eat the boxed lunch I bought at the convenience store, have a few beers, and fall asleep in front of the TV.

They stepped out of the elevator and left through the front door of the building.

"This will do," Moriizumi said flatly, glancing over her shoulder.

"No, I should see this through," Kanako insisted with an exaggerated wave of her hand. "Is this your car?" she asked, quickly sliding herself into the passenger seat of Moriizumi's van.

"Hold on, you're starting to scare me here."

But Kanako didn't care that Moriizumi was beginning to look more than a little annoyed. "It's okay. This was always the plan. Besides, I'll be finished for the day once it's all over and done with."

"That's not what I mean."

"Really, it's alright."

Kanako was beginning to understand that the instructions she had received weren't a request from the disposal company, but rather a direct order from Chief Mochida. That man had a habit of phrasing things as if they were someone else's idea.

"I've had that phone since forever. I want to stay with it till the end." That was a lie, but her mouth seemed to be moving of its own accord. "More importantly, though, because of all the data and personal information on it, it has to be—er, hold on a second, let me check the exact words—completely *destroyed and incinerated*. If it isn't, I'll be held accountable."

Moriizumi didn't understand half of what Kanako was saying, but at this rate, they would be here forever.

"Suit yourself then," she said as she started the engine.

Kanako stole a sideways glance at Moriizumi's funeral clothes. The rear compartment was filled with cardboard boxes, each containing old telephones. Not just one or two, either. There had to be at least a dozen of them.

"Are you supposed to dress like that when you lay a phone to rest?" she asked.

"No," Moriizumi answered, clearly annoyed. "This is for my day job. I haven't had time to change yet."

"Your day job?"

The car pulled onto the highway running under the Metropolitan Expressway. Amber streetlights on the other side of the windshield illuminated their faces every couple of seconds.

"My family runs a funeral home. Sometimes, they ask me to come in and help. I'm an only child, and my parents are getting on in years, so I can't exactly say no."

"Oh. I see."

"And you, Fuyuki—you work at a call center?"

"Huh? How do you know my name?"

"What kind of question is that? You gave me your business card and signed for the phone."

So she did *read it.*

Kanako was more than a little surprised, but when she took a good, careful look at Moriizumi's profile, she finally understood. She was clearly older than first impressions might lead one to believe.

"Kanako Fuyuki, desk twenty-five on the fourth-floor call center of the Tokyo No. 3 Consultation Room. Right?" Moriizumi seemed to have the details on the business card down pat.

Kanako was impressed. She was clearly the real thing, a bona fide professional—far more experienced than Goto, in any event.

"So, where is it? The telephone . . . I guess you would call it a graveyard?"

Moriizumi let out a loud snort. "There's no such thing."

"But isn't it going to be destroyed?"

"That's not our job."

"Then how . . . "

"We just delete the data and send it on to a recycling company. We don't destroy them, and we don't incinerate them either."

"You don't smash them with a hammer or anything?"

"No."

"Oh."

Kanako almost burst into laughter. She herself didn't know why.

"Huh?" she startled, hurrying to put on a serious face and sit up straight. "Wait. Then where are we going?"

Kanako got out of the car, though she regretted it almost immediately. She had clearly slipped up here, but she didn't want to inconvenience Moriizumi any more than she already had.

"My place is just around here," she lied, asking to be dropped off at an unfamiliar intersection.

Kanako suddenly remembered something the woman who ran the bar once said to her. "You know, you're a lot like your brother. Blood is blood, I suppose. You're impulsive, free-willed—pig-headed, even—always out looking for something. Before you know it, you'll probably end up lost yourself."

She stood at a deserted intersection in the middle of the night, her eyes watching the traffic lights alternate between green and red.

"Where am I?"

Not a single car passed by. The town was devoid of sound, as if someone had suddenly turned the volume down to zero.

Kanako stood in the center of that silence.

"What should I do now?"

She reached into her jacket pocket, her fingers brushing

against Moriizumi's business card, the one she had just received, before finding another that had been in there quite a bit longer.

Blackbird—the night taxi.

Anytime, anywhere, it read.

Eighteen Keys

Matsui glanced at the clock. It was 1:00 A.M.

A young man, alone, was standing on the dark sidewalk on a backstreet near Izumo Bridge, bashfully raising a hand into the air. Something about his figure struck Matsui as furtive, so he stopped the car carefully, checking to see if anyone was watching.

There was no one else in sight.

He was in the middle of a lonely stretch of road between a residential area and a subway railyard.

"Ah, thank goodness!" the youth exclaimed as he got into the car. Pausing to take a deep breath, he added in a clear voice: "To Shinjuku."

"Where in Shinjuku?" Matsui asked, glancing at him in the rearview mirror.

"An all-night movie theater. Hold on a sec. Er . . . The Shinjuku Comet Cinema," the man stammered, nodding as he read from his cellphone screen.

The bright light illuminated his face. At first glance, Matsui had taken him to be in his early twenties, but on closer inspection, he could well have been over thirty.

"A movie at this time of night?"

Matsui knew that it wasn't his place to ask questions, but he was curious. Part of him wanted to pull at the threads of this story.

"Yep," the man answered unconcernedly. "I've had a change of plans."

Relief washed over Matsui.

Though he had never personally had any serious problems, there was an ironclad rule among taxi drivers that if you picked up a customer at an *irregular* place, at an *irregular* hour, you should at least try to work out what kind of person they were before setting off.

First of all, you had to check that they didn't have a screw or two loose, to make sure that they weren't out looking for a fight or else planning to do something reckless out of desperation.

That being said, it wasn't good manners to eyeball customers, even through a rearview mirror. It was even worse to let them distract you from the road. In any event, Matsui could tell at a glance whether or not a customer was the type to cause trouble.

The youth—or rather, the man who came across as a youth—looked a little worn down, but he didn't seem overly suspicious. Matsui had succeeded in revealing the outlines of his story, but he wasn't sure whether he ought to hazard continuing the conversation.

At that moment—

"I've been walking all day," the man explained. "I'm beat. I just want somewhere to get some shuteye."

"Ah," Matsui nodded, though he still didn't quite understand.

Maybe he wanted to sleep in the taxi? So Matsui thought, at first, before realizing that the man was responding to his question. In other words, he probably meant to get some sleep in the movie theater.

"Does your job have you doing a lot of walking?" Matsui asked.

"Yeah," the man answered. "But I had a day off today," he continued, as if taking the first part back. "I finally got around to doing something I'd been putting off for a long time."

He certainly did have a young man's way of talking, Matsui thought to himself.

Matsui kept his eyes ahead of him, doing his best not to let his passenger distract him from the road. Finally emerging from the dark residential area onto a major road, he spotted a traffic sign pointing to Shinjuku.

"So you were planning to walk about all day long?" he asked, turning his attention back to the man's story as he rounded a corner.

"Yeah. I finally managed to finish a job."

"Not very good weather for it today, though?"

"No. It was cloudy all day."

Being a nighttime driver, Matsui slept through most of the day, so he only learned about the weather on the evening news.

"It looked like it might start pouring down any minute," he said, repeating secondhand what he had heard on the forecast.

The man gave his head a slight shake. "I . . . I'm not very good with rain. I've had a few traumatic experiences, you might say . . . "

"You have bad memories about the rain?"

"No, not memories, exactly. Whenever it rains, there's always one of those *incidents*, you see."

"Incidents?" Matsui repeated, aware that his right eyebrow had just twitched slightly.

Moving around on foot all day, talking about *incidents*—was the man a detective? He didn't look the part, but even so . . .

"Have you ever heard of Detective Shuro?" the man asked.

"Hmm?" Matsui wasn't sure whether he had misheard. "I'm sorry, could you say that again?" he asked, peering into the rearview mirror.

The man was staring vacantly outside the window at the stream of late-night stores. "Detective Shuro. You haven't heard the name?"

"Ah." Matsui tilted his head to one side. "Sorry, I can't say it rings a bell."

"That's fine. I guess you could say I'm . . . Well . . . Shuro is a movie character, you see?"

"Ah. You're an actor?"

"Uh, well . . . "

"I see, I see. My apologies. You might not guess it, but I have lots of friends and customers in the film industry, so I've picked up my own fair share of movie trivia. Though I've never heard of anything called *Detective Shuro* before."

"Well, it's a series of relatively minor B-movies," the man interrupted. That wasn't quite true, but it would be a pain to have to go into any great detail. "As you've probably guessed, I play the detective named Shuro."

Yes, that would do.

After all, it wasn't all that far from the truth.

A long, long time ago, at his father's urging, he *had* been a child actor, appearing in several films.

But not anymore. Now, he really was a detective. A reasonably well-known detective, he liked to think. Yet this taxi driver, despite claiming to be a movie buff, hadn't responded to his name at all.

Very well. The media liked to make its jokes, labelling him a so-called *great* detective, like some children's television character, yet the fact remained that he *had* solved more than his fair share of cases. Many of those incidents had become the talk of the town, even being adapted into novels and movies.

With his current fame, he made a point of telling people that his real given name was in fact Shuro, albeit written with the characters for *hemp palm*. Over time, however, what had begun as a fictional moniker written purely phonetically had become his own nickname, and people called out to him on the streets not with his surname, but with a short, succinct *Shuro!*

"Apologies for the misunderstanding," the driver said with a bow of his head.

Shuro felt himself overcome by the rare urge to go on in greater detail. He was unusually talkative today. He wouldn't normally divulge this much, especially not to a stranger.

"They weren't shooting any scenes today."

Shuro's eyes caught the light of streetlamps passing by at regular intervals.

"So I just spent the day wandering around Tokyo."

"Oh? Did you just move here, by any chance?"

"No. Far from it."

Shuro glanced at the driver's face in the mirror. His voice alone was enough to leave a good impression. He seemed like a decent fellow.

This was one of his detective habits, gauging a person's disposition based solely on his first impressions. If he was at the scene of a crime, he could sometimes judge whether or not someone was the culprit simply by looking at them. First impressions were important. Of course, it was necessary to investigate the suspects thoroughly, but it was equally true that good detectives had sufficient experience to come to preliminary conclusions based on intuition alone.

"I was born and raised in Tokyo."

For the time being, Shuro had deemed Matsui a good man.

"But I'm a constant mover," he continued, turning his gaze back to the dark street outside. "I'm always changing neighborhoods, though I like to stay in Tokyo."

Maybe he was talking too much. But for some reason, he couldn't stop himself.

"Today, I was checking out all the apartments I used to live in."

"Ah." Matsui almost bought the story, but the thought of walking around all day struck him as *irregular*. It just didn't sit well.

"From my first apartment to the one I'm living in now, I've moved nineteen times."

Yes, *very* unusual.

Torn between suspicion and curiosity, Matsui voiced his thoughts. "How can you remember that many of them?"

"I have the keys," the man said, raising his voice slightly. "Apart from the one for my current apartment, there are eighteen others." He sounded almost like he was boasting at the end there.

"I see."

Matsui didn't really understand what exactly he was nodding along to. Essentially, the man was saying that he had kept the keys to all the apartments he had ever lived in.

No, wait. He stopped himself. Come to think of it, he himself had changed residence on three separate occasions, and he too had kept the old keys in the back of a drawer in his office, even though he knew he couldn't use them anymore.

"Those eighteen keys are probably useless now. There's not a door in the whole wide world they can open anymore. Or at least, there shouldn't be."

Matsui studied Shuro in the rearview mirror. For a moment, their eyes met—truly met. In his line of work, he sometimes looked into the eyes of his passengers to get an inkling of their real selves. This man, this purported actor, claimed that he played the role of a detective.

Normally, someone like that would in all likelihood be a professional burglar or something else of the sort—but if he was talking about minor B-movies, then his claims weren't implausible. Or else had he been walking around town all day long jangling those eighteen sets of keys in order to break into one empty apartment after another?

"What kind of movie is it?" Matsui tried asking.

"Eh?" Shuro seemed puzzled by the sudden shift back to

the previous topic. "Well, the detective is the main character, and—"

"No, not that one," Matsui interrupted. "What kind of film are you going to see tonight?"

"Ah." Shuro's voice faltered. "Well, I'm planning to sleep through it anyway. It could be anything, for all I care. But it's an old Japanese movie, about a thief. Not a detective . . . " He trailed off toward the end.

"A thief?" Matsui exclaimed in alarm, before inwardly reprimanding himself.

A taxi driver shouldn't give way to panic in this kind of situation. Even if the person behind him was a violent criminal, he had to keep calm so that they wouldn't notice. It was an elementary mistake, betraying that you had caught on by failing to control your voice.

Shuro, however, seemed unperturbed. "To tell you the truth, my father used to be what they call a phantom thief. Only a few people knew," he said, nodding somberly.

"Oh?" Matsui chose his next words carefully. "A phantom thief? Like in *The Fiend with Twenty Faces*?"

Yes, he remembered. That was what it was called.

The book *The Car is the Color of the Sky* had set him on the path of becoming a taxi driver. Afterward, he had found himself hooked on Edogawa Rampo's *Boys' Detectives Club* series, of which *The Fiend with Twenty Faces* was the first volume.

His passenger looked like a youth, but he wasn't quite a young man. He claimed to be playing the part of a detective, but then confessed to being the son of a thief. On top of that, he lied by saying that he couldn't open any doors, yet he had eighteen keys hidden in his pocket.

"Don't tell me *you're* the Fiend with Twenty Faces?"

The Fiend, huh?
Shuro hid his face, biting down on his laughter.

Whenever Shuro told someone he was a constant mover, he would make up some random number, telling them that he had twenty-six or thirty-eight keys or even more. This time, for the first time, he had actually rummaged through his box for all of them, counting eighteen in total. They were all similar in shape and design, plain and silver-colored—but all he had to do was hold them in his hand to relive the way they had turned in their locks, the color of the doors, even the rooms beyond once they swung open.

There was no doubt it was these talents that had made him a first-class detective. However, he lacked the sense of humor necessary to adopt the mantle of the Fiend of Twenty Faces.

Even if completely misguided, the comparison was an amusing one. Combining the eighteen apartments, the one where he presently lived, and the house where he was born, now long gone, there were exactly twenty.

Thus far, his life had certainly been a story of twenty chapters. Visiting the eighteen apartments on his day-long tour of Tokyo had borne that home to him.

There had been one particular twist during his day's wanderings.

He had visited his old apartment in Shimokitazawa first, where he had lived before moving to his current home. From there, he retraced his previous residences as if swimming upstream in the flow of time, making his way to a building called Kofukuso in Daitabashi, then to the Mikazuki apartment building in Asagaya.

When he reached the sixth apartment, he found that the building was no longer there.

He had kept the eighteen keys as good luck charms, but he had no intention of actually inserting them into the locks to chance whether they would really open the doors. He just wanted to reminisce, to retrace the footsteps of a life moving too quickly from roost to roost.

What mattered were the memories of his time living in each place, so it didn't really matter whether the buildings had been demolished. His powers of recollection were exemplary, and holding the keys in his hand made them come back to him all the more clearly.

The keys were precisely that.

For instance, it was while living in his eleventh apartment that he solved a series of cold cases and first made a name for himself as a detective. The building was still there, just a ten-minute walk south of Gakugei University Station. It had been a tiny six-mat room, just a hundred square feet in size, complete with a small loft. The apartment, the leftmost unit on the second floor, was now occupied by another tenant. That was only natural—yet Shuro still had the key from his time living there. Now, it belonged to someone else. It all struck him as frustratingly discordant.

Before that, during his time in his seventh apartment, he had been a magician calling himself the Mighty Tashiro. However, he had only ever performed on stage as a sideshow at banquets held by local factories and merchants' associations. Most of the time, he practiced sleight-of-hand table magic in a corner of some bar. He was self-taught. Magic tricks had been a hobby of his since he was a child, though he couldn't possibly make a living from it. He worked at a nearby canning factory during the day, surviving off a diet of canned goods.

He didn't have a great many fond memories from that time, but his knowledge of magic tricks had certainly come in handy after he became a detective. In fact, he believed it was precisely thanks to that experience that he had become the detective he was today. After all, the goals were much the same. How do you distract people from what you don't want them to see? What kind of deceptions are most effective?

There was a secret to every magic trick, an answer cleverly concealed behind a web of complex deceits. Even today, his faith in the simple truth that every mystery must have a solution lay beneath his deductions.

He could never have imagined becoming a magician, let alone a detective, during his time at his third apartment, the Mizoguchi building in Ekoda. Changing part-time jobs at roughly two-month intervals, he had lived a precarious hand-to-mouth existence, with no clear vision of the future. The rent had been cheap enough, seeing as the place didn't even come with a bath, but it was no problem on his part to frequent the public bathhouse next to the shopping arcade. Both buildings were long gone, but it was at that bathhouse where he met the men who taught him sleight-of-hand, setting him on the path of performing magic tricks at local bars.

It all seemed so surreal.

Well, if I retrace my steps far enough, eventually, I'll come to that . . .

Matsui's taxi, the color of the night sky, was quickly approaching Shinjuku.

Shinjuku was often said to be Tokyo's sleepless fortress, but even its network of all-hour blinding lights was smaller than it once was. While the vehicle may have technically entered the district, their surroundings were still dark, black trees casting deep shadows into the interior of the car.

Matsui continued to ponder as he concentrated on his driving.

The man in the back seat had called himself an actor playing a detective, but as the conversation progressed, he had begun to talk as if he truly was a detective.

Maybe he *did* have a few screws loose.

Matsui probably shouldn't have paid his story much heed, but more than all that stuff about detectives and investigations, the words *retrace your steps* had struck a chord with him.

Matsui had memories of his own that he would like to go

back to, insignificant though they were. One of these days, he knew, he would have to face up to them all. But for now, he had managed to convince himself that it was enough to drive around at night, leaving the destination up to the customer without deciding for himself where he wanted to go.

He was constantly on the move—almost as if trying to avoid facing something.

"Me too, actually."

All of a sudden, he felt like something had come undone inside him, like a tight shoelace abruptly unraveling.

Maybe I should talk about it, he thought.

No. He *did* want to talk about it. He was certain.

But the taxi had already arrived at Shinjuku, less than two minutes away from the movie theater.

"I also used to live in an apartment without a bathtub," he said. "A passenger I picked up recently happened to be from the same area, and when I passed through, I found that the public bathhouse I used to go to was gone, like it had never existed."

His expression sour, he forced out a weak laugh.

To tell the truth, Shuro knew that he was putting on a front—to himself more than the driver—when he said that any movie would do.

Similarly, all that about just wanting to get some shuteye was him doing his best to play it off.

The screening started at 1:50 A.M.

From the very beginning, watching this film was meant to be the highlight of the day. If he followed the keys back to the last one, which he had added to his collection later, he would end up at the estate where he had lived with his father—a house built by a lifelong supporting actor, appearing in over five hundred separate films.

At the end of all those keys was that house.

And the film in question was the sole exception in his father's career of playing minor supporting characters, the one work in which he had taken the lead role—*Silva the Phantom Thief*.

That was the movie being shown unnoticed in the dead of night.

Shuro had happened to see it listed on the daily program as part of a special screening event titled *Unknown Masterpieces*. It was being shown only once, a couple of hours after midnight. It had never been released on home video, and while his father had spoken about the film on a great many occasions, this would be Shuro's first time seeing it for himself.

He still didn't know precisely what role his father had in it.

What little he knew about it he had picked up by chance several years ago. Before becoming a detective, probably around the time of his eighth apartment, he had found a synopsis of *Silva the Phantom Thief* in a used bookstore. After reading it, he had come back disappointed. While the thief was certainly the main character, he had been outsmarted by the detective toward the end.

So why don't I become a detective too? Shuro had thought at the time.

A real detective, not an actor playing a part. One who solved truly formidable cases. That would show him.

If they had arrived at the cinema a little bit later, Shuro might have shared all this with Matsui. But when he looked out the window, he saw that the streets were full of people, even at this late hour.

"We've arrived," Matsui said, waking him as if from a dream.

As he stepped out of the taxi and stood in front of the movie theater, the sky, which had been threatening rain all day, finally gave way, dousing Shuro in the one thing he hated most.

The water was strangely warm—gentle, even.

But he wasn't exaggerating when he said that rain had a

tendency to usher in criminal activity. Whether a downpour or a light drizzle, rain never failed to bring a fresh case. Shuro had no idea why, but most of the cases he had taken on had occurred on rainy days.

Perhaps the weather had a way of playing on people's minds, of pushing them to extremes.

The theater was precisely that—complete with curtain and stage—and was located a short distance from the train station. It looked like it had just opened. Shuro was pleasantly surprised to see the owner's spirit in every aspect of the building, from its appearance, which reminded him of cinemas from a bygone era, to its program, featuring an extensive collection of films that had seldom seen the light of day.

If he had one complaint, it was that there was no old-fashioned ticket window. Instead, tickets were issued by a device in the lobby that could easily have been mistaken for an arcade machine. The machine controlled all aspects of bookings and ticket purchases, and you could even choose your desired seat from a chart on the monitor.

While a detective by trade, Shuro was incredibly clumsy when it came to such basic things as buying a ticket or paying a utility bill.

But even he knew that this late-night screening was particularly unusual. The ticket machine seemed to be connected to the internet, and it looked like you could buy seats ahead of time. There was no need to purchase them at the entrance, as Shuro was doing.

If a film was popular, it was entirely possible that the seats might be booked out well before the screening. Yet not a single seat for *Silva the Phantom Thief* was taken, even though the movie would be starting in just five minutes.

That the film was being shown this way, that the date of the screening had coincided with his day off, that all indications were he would be watching it alone—and above all, that he would finally be able to see his father's greatest work—perhaps this mysterious chain of events could itself be termed an *incident*.

"I don't suppose you could pick me up after it's finished?" Shuro asked as he stepped out of the vehicle.

"Of course," Matsui was quick to answer.

"It goes until three thirty, so I'll call around then."

"Understood."

Matsui searched his pocket, before handing him a business card with his cellphone number.

If he picked up another passenger who needed to make his way across the city, he would have no choice but to turn Shuro down. But for some reason, even though the rain was coming down hard, he found no other customers. After a short while, he decided he might as well head back to the theater.

Where would Shuro want to go after the screening?

Would he ask to be driven back to his nineteenth apartment? Or maybe he would seek out another movie theater running a late-night screening? It would depend on how long the trip took, but if it was going to be longer than fifteen minutes, Matsui was thinking about opening up about himself.

Perhaps it was an exaggeration to consider something as trivial as the night's events *fate*. In any event, he would first have to work out whether the man calling himself Shuro was an actor or a real detective. If he *was* a detective, he might even hear him out—and maybe he could help locate *her*.

Matsui felt as if a locked door had been opened for him. Until now, he had been going about his job in the faint hope that he might accidentally bump into her again. He had never considered the possibility of hiring a detective.

To be perfectly honest, it didn't even matter if the man was a real detective or merely playing the part. It would be enough if he just lent a sympathetic ear.

Fate, however, was a fickle thing.

Four o'clock came and went, and Shuro still hadn't called. At four thirty, Matsui shook his head, deciding to put the whole affair behind him.

At the very least, the faintest flicker of hope had been rekindled inside him. In his mind's eye, a memory that he had kept locked away for he couldn't remember how long came alive again—the sight of her face staring blankly out the window from inside the car.

Just as he managed to regain his composure, his cellphone rang. "Yes?" he said, picking up.

"Hello?" came an unfamiliar female voice. "It's Fuyuki."

Her words seemed to reach back to him from far beyond the dark of night.

HAM AND EGGS

The clock hands pointed to 1:00 A.M.

Six and a half hours to go. An eternity.

"Step on it," the four women mumbled as they sipped glasses of beer and shochu while stealing glances at the customers. "Gotta fuel up."

They weren't drinking, not as such.

It was a fine line, but all four of them understood that they weren't allowed to drink at work, though they had never formally agreed to this rule.

They were a cohesive team, yet their decision to open an all-night diner together had come about entirely by chance.

All four of them had somewhat similar personalities—they were all frankly spoken, they all wore their hair short, and they all hated slothfulness more than anything else. At the same time, they all found it stifling when people were overly rigid, so they would sooner take the quick and easy path than aim for perfection.

Perhaps it was because of these traits, or else the continued rise of chain restaurants, that they had all chosen to close their old establishments and set out as unrestrained as the ocean waves.

They weren't originally close friends. Their old restaurants had been located far apart, and they didn't communicate all that frequently.

Kisa, the oldest, had once worked at the same izakaya bar as Yorie, the youngest. Fumina, the shrewdest of the four, had been in the same high school class as the remaining woman, Ayano, and had eaten at Kisa's diner on several occasions. Ayano and Yorie lived not too far from one another, and had met several times at a Chinese noodle shop in the local shopping arcade.

While they weren't particularly close, they would say hello whenever they bumped into each other. Those brief greetings gradually developed into longer conversations, until before they knew it, they learned that each had their own eatery and that they were all facing the same difficult business conditions.

After learning about their shared circumstances, they took their distance for a while. Eventually, through the deluge of gossip and rumor making its way around town, they discovered that they were all planning on closing up shop around the same time.

"Why don't we open a new diner together, then?"

Exactly who came up with this suggestion remained a mystery to this very day. They all assumed that it was Kisa, the oldest, and yet—

"It wasn't me," she responded with an angry snort.

"Fumina, then?" Yorie wondered aloud.

Yet Fumina, the shortest, waved a hand in front of her face. "No, not me," she maintained.

The other two insisted that it wasn't them either, with all four left thinking it wasn't *their* idea. Solidarity was their strength, and they were united in their vehement denial.

And so the four of them were approaching five years working together, never having had any major disputes in the running of their diner, the Yotsukado.

Matsui liked to think of the Yotsukado as his *special diner*.

In this case, *special* meant that it was the best of the best, a sanctuary that he spoke of to no one. If he could help it, he would eat there every morning. There were always a good many customers, and if it became any more popular, he might have to give up enjoying the restaurant's delicious set meals for himself. That was why he kept his lips sealed.

On nights when a reservation he was counting on fell through after 4:00 A.M., he would make his way to the Yotsukado to try to clear his head.

Tonight was no different.

When he stopped to think about it, Shuro had been a strange passenger. As his story progressed, he implied that he was a detective—and not just any detective, a *great* detective. Was Matsui supposed to take him at his word?

If he really was all he made himself out to be, Matsui would have liked to discuss his own situation with him. He had been on the verge of opening up about a matter that he had never discussed with anyone, of saying *There's someone I want you to track down.*

After four o'clock came and went and the expected phone call didn't materialize, Matsui realized he had been given the slip. He drove back to the movie theater a few times, but there was no sign of the purported detective.

This wasn't an altogether unusual occurrence. He had been more hopeful than usual this time around because he had his own agenda, but it wasn't uncommon for reservations to be cancelled without notice—in other words, by failing to call.

There's no use stewing over it. I might as well head to the Yotsukado, he decided, changing the sign on his windshield from *Vacant* to *Out of Service.*

"Maybe I'll call it a day . . . " he mumbled into the windshield to no one in particular.

He felt vaguely queasy, as if some unidentified thought was stuck in his throat. At times like this, you could lose your focus and end up in a traffic accident.

"Alright."

Giving his head a firm shake to clear his thoughts, he set out for the intersection in Katatokicho and the Yotsukado diner.

Her face seemed to keep flashing before him, leaving him unable to concentrate on his driving.

Just as he straightened his back and shook his head once more, his cellphone began to ring.

The name Yotsukado, meaning *crossroads*, came from the fact that the building was located on a four-way intersection. However, back when they had first decided that this was the property they wanted, the four women had been racked with indecision.

"I don't care about the name," one of them had said.

"I'm fine just calling it *Diner*."

"A fancy name is all well and good, but it won't change the quality of the food."

"Yep. Taste is what matters most."

"Right, right."

"But a restaurant with no name?"

"I see what you mean . . . "

"We have to make it easy for customers to remember."

"Well, it's at an intersection. That's the main landmark, right? How about Yotsukado, then?"

"Yotsukado? Not bad."

And so it was decided.

In spite of this, back when they had each opened their own restaurants, they had been incredibly particular about choosing the right name.

"I remember stewing over it for more than a month," Kisa said with a faraway look in her eyes.

"Me too."

"Tell me about it."

"I thought it was *so* important to pick the right one."

The bitter pill of having to shutter their old shops had imparted them all with a sense of resignation, and so during their evening preparation, while gearing up for the day, they often talked about throwing in the towel.

"I just don't care anymore."

"I know what you mean."

They would be focusing on the knives and chopsticks in their hands, the conversation slowly coming into being as they pulled at a new thread each time a memory gradually revealed itself.

"I'd like some time to myself for once."

"Tell me about it."

"I know . . . "

"Yeah. I used to care more about making the most of my time off."

"Me too."

"Do your job well, and live fulfilled during your downtime, huh?"

"Exactly."

"There's no such thing."

"Nope."

"I don't think I've ever had a *fulfilling* day off, come to think of it."

"I wouldn't call running a diner all that *fulfilling* either, though?"

"Not even this one?"

Silence fell over the four women for a long moment.

"I mean, I've given up on it all."

"Yep. I've basically stopped trying."

"Hopes and dreams, huh . . . "

"Hey, you know? Edoites are always quick to give in. That's basically their sole merit."

"Huh? Their sole merit?"

"It means they know what matters."

"Are you guys even real Edoites, though?"

"*I* am. Tokyo born and bred."

"Me too."

The four of them paused for a moment, each nodding in agreement.

"It's just common sense."

"*What's* common sense?"

"They say Edoites can never follow through with anything."

Once more, they each swallowed their words, moving their hands in stony silence.

The sound of knives clacking on cutting boards, of food simmering in pots seemed to stretch out all around.

"It's Fuyuki," came the calm voice of the woman on the other end of the line.

She spoke as if she knew him, but Matsui couldn't stick a face to the name.

"Kanako Fuyuki."

"Um . . . I'm sorry?"

"Oh. Excuse me. I helped with the . . . er . . . the loquats."

"Ah." That word was enough to jolt his memories. "The loquat thief."

"Yes."

All of a sudden, they both burst into laughter.

"How can I help?"

"If you're not busy, could you come pick me up? The thing is, though, I don't really know where I am."

"Of course," Matsui said, pulling over to the side of the road and switching on his GPS navigation. "Look for a lamppost. There should be an address written on it."

"A lamppost?"

Matsui could hear her gasping for breath as she looked around.

"I—I've found one. Um . . . "

Hearing her recite the address in her crisp, clear voice, Matsui's memories began to come back to him. *Right, didn't she say that she worked at a call center?*

"Number two-dash-six," he repeated, confirming the exact address.

According to his GPS, she wasn't all that far away.

"I can reach you in a couple of minutes. Is that okay?"

"Yes please. I greatly appreciate it."

"I'll be there soon."

No sooner did Matsui hang up than Kanako Fuyuki felt a tickle of relief, chuckling to herself with a lop-sided smile.

Soon, huh?

She was starving, she realized with a sigh. She would normally grab a boxed convenience store lunch after work, or else go to an all-night restaurant for a light meal. Tonight, however, had been one surprise after another, and time had gotten away from her.

Maybe I should get a bite to eat before heading home.

"But you know, there's gotta be at least *one* thing you don't wanna give up?"

"Not for me, there isn't."

The four women were standing behind the counter, each seeing to her own tasks as they spoke in muted conversation, just as they had done earlier in the evening while preparing the night's food.

"There has to be *something*, though?"

"Like what?"

"A man, maybe?"

It was already four-thirty, and there were hardly ever customers at that hour. The diner closed at seven-thirty in the morning, but once five-thirty rolled around, they would be inundated with old folks coming in for breakfast, men finishing their night shifts, and taxi drivers who had been working through the night.

The hour and a half after four o'clock was the most peaceful period of the night, a chance for the four of them to catch their breath. It also gave them ample time to prepare the second batch of food for the morning customers.

"Love? Romance?"

"I gave *them* up ages ago."

"You can say that again."

"I'm done with them all."

"Men just string you along."

"But still . . . "

"Yeah, yeah. You don't have to say it. I know."

"We're the kind to go all in. The four of us, when we set our minds on something, we get totally absorbed in it."

"That's true. If we were any different, we wouldn't have dreamed of opening diners on our own."

"Come to think of it, we did pretty well. Seeing as we did it all ourselves."

"Despite being Edoites, right?"

"We really threw ourselves into it, huh?"

"Eh? What do you mean? With a guy?"

"That too. I get lost in someone, and they get lost in me too."

"Same here. He'll be all crazy about me, and we'll both end up miserable. Because I'm too invested in the store."

"It was laid out pretty clearly to me. I could either keep the restaurant or keep the man. I picked the restaurant. I had to shutter it in the end, though, so maybe I should have picked the guy."

"Do you regret it?"

"No. I don't *do* regret."

"Yeah. When you hear the word *regret*, that's basically assuming things always go well, right? But come on, that's not possible. Something *always* goes wrong. If you had gone with the guy, it would've been something else. So there's no point second guessing yourself."

"I guess. So regrets are a lot like hopes and dreams?"

"Exactly. It's all a fantasy, thinking I would have been happy if only I'd done this or that."

"What about you, Ayano? You've been pretty quiet for a while now."

"Don't tell me you really *do* have regrets?"

"No. It's not that . . . "

"But?"

She might not have *regrets*, as such, but there *was* something weighing on her mind.

Ayano's old diner had been located on the northern edge of Tokyo. In the beginning, men from nearby factories would drop by to eat day and night. It was a profitable enough business. Soon afterward, however, the factories closed their doors, her customers dwindled, and it all became too expensive to keep going.

Her only real reason to keep the diner running had been a man named Tashiro. At least, that was his surname. She didn't know his first name. His hair was always a mess, and he wore the same clothes all year round. His face was stubbly, and there was a crack on the edge of one of his glasses lenses.

He can't have been all that well off.

He always ordered the ham-and-eggs set. Though the cheapest meal on the menu, it was a well-balanced assortment of meat, eggs, and vegetables.

"At this point, my body is basically entirely made up of your ham-and-eggs set."

He had a radiant, childlike smile. Ayano didn't know much about his everyday life or troubles, but when she spoke with him in her diner, his eyes were always carefree and gentle.

That was probably what first drew her to him.

Were these her maternal instincts at work? She felt like it would be perfect, the natural way of things to spend her life in the company of someone like this.

She tried discussing it with Haruka, a close friend from her student days.

"That's just how it is, isn't it?" Haruka had responded casually. "You felt the same about your restaurant, right? It's the root of all this."

"What is?"

"You want to be like a mom to people."

"Huh? Me?"

"You just haven't realized it for yourself yet. I mean, *I* don't feel that way. Not in the slightest. As far as I'm concerned, it's a pain just making my own meals. I really admire you, you know? You cook for everyone. You're basically the mother of this whole neighborhood."

Am I really, though? Ayano still wasn't entirely sure.

She couldn't say for sure, but if it *was* true . . .

In that case, maybe I should have done more. Maybe I should have asked him . . .

If he had kept coming to the diner for a little while longer, maybe things could have been different. But he stopped dropping by a couple of months before she made the call to close up shop for good. He simply stopped coming in one day. She knew that he lived somewhere in the neighborhood, so either he had moved away, or he had found somewhere better to eat.

It's like it never happened, she thought with a pang in her chest.

She still didn't know whether her interest in him had been serious or just a vain fancy, but the person with whom she had considered spending the rest of her life had suddenly vanished. Up until that moment, she had seen him each and every day. Then, just like that, the connection was lost.

With that, Ayano realized that this was what it meant to run a restaurant.

People were fickle creatures, and human connections were always fleeting. So she carved the experience into her heart as a lesson—if she was to survive in this town, her best option was simply to give up.

And yet . . .

"Hmm?" Kisa glanced up as a customer stepped into the diner. "Oh?" she exclaimed.

"Eh?" "Huh?" "What?" chimed in the other three.

"Welcome," Kisa said in greeting.

It was Matsui and Kanako.

The four women checked the clock. Right, it wasn't out of place for Matsui to stop by at this hour. What *was* unusual, they all thought with excitement, was that he was with someone else—a woman at that.

Pretending to busy themselves preparing for the morning rush, the four women tuned their ears to the table where Matsui and his guest sat chatting quietly.

"To tell you the truth, I've never brought a guest here before," Matsui confessed.

"Oh? I had no idea," Kanako answered. She had been in the midst of reaching the cup of hojicha tea brought by Yorie, but her hand came to a stop.

"Yes. It's like this place is my secret hideaway. Ms. Fuyuki, I—"

"Kanako is fine. That's what everyone else calls me."

Kanako didn't like standing on ceremony. She could get along with anyone, loosening up around an acquaintance of five minutes as if she had known them for as many years. This relaxed nature of hers was contagious, with people quickly opening up to her in turn. Sometimes, she couldn't help but wonder if she had developed this skill through her work, or whether it simply came naturally to her. Probably both.

For Matsui's part, he could clearly recall the night when Kanako had offered him a glass of her home-brewed loquat wine. But even so, he was taken aback when she asked him to address her on a first-name basis. That being said, he was no stranger to dealing with all manner of customers, and he knew from years of experience that in such cases, it was always best to respect the other party's request.

"Very well," he said, sipping at his hojicha tea. "I was already thinking of stopping by here before you called, Kanako."

"You were? Thank goodness. I was getting hungry myself."

"That should be my line. I was just thinking about calling it a day and grabbing a bite."

"Sorry for calling you out like this at the end of your day."

"Not at all. It's my job. It's just that when someone lights a fire of hunger inside you—hold on. People don't say that, do they? Light a fire of hunger?"

The four women at the counter quickly looked down, doing their best to stifle their laughter.

Typical Matsui.

He's always like this.

He's got his own way of talking.

He comes out with the strangest lines.

Looking over the menu, Matsui went straight to his usual choice, the classic B Set.

"Hmm . . . I don't know . . . " Kanako seemed to have trouble deciding, but finally called out to Yorie with a smile: "The ham-and-egg set."

"Hey," Yorie whispered as soon as she returned to the counter. "That woman, she's *gorgeous*. And she smells nice too."

"Has Matsui fallen in love?" Kisa wondered aloud.

"That has to be it," Fumina exclaimed. "Look at them. They're lovestruck."

The three continued to whisper among themselves.

Ayano was the only one with any real connection to the ham-and-egg set. "Of all things," she murmured under her breath, too low for any of the others to overhear. She strained to listen in on the conversation.

"That customer I was telling you about earlier . . . " Matsui's voice trailed off a little.

"The detective?" Kanako asked, thinking back to the story he had told her on the way to the diner.

It seemed a customer had made a reservation, only to fail to follow through.

"He sounded like the real thing. Have you ever heard of him? Detective Shuro?" Matsui asked.

Kanako shook her head. "No."

"He mentioned some movies based on a series of novels about his cases," Matsui told her.

This was enough to jolt her memory. "Ah, *that* Shuro?"

She had gone to a cinema complex in Shinjuku on her day off last week, and recalled seeing a trailer for the next installment in the *Detective Shuro* series, due for release in the spring. There had hardly been any actual clips from the film, however, just ostentatious music set to taglines like *Unraveling cold cases*, *Heart-pounding mysteries*, *Countless adventures*, and *Stay tuned!*

"At least the movie part must have been true." She took another sip at her tea, her eyes narrowing in pleasure. "This is delicious."

"I see. I hadn't heard of them." Matsui stroked his chin with his fingertips. The amount of stubble all but told him it would soon be morning.

Indeed, the street outside the glass door was slowly lightening, the town bathed in a dark shade of greenish blue.

"So he really was a great detective?"

"Maybe it was a valuable experience, then?" Kanako wondered, gazing out the window.

With the two having fallen suddenly silent, the four women paused at their cooking to check on the situation. The customers were staring outside, a somber feeling having fallen over them. The four women likewise looked outside.

Night was coming to a close, the quietest hour in busy Tokyo.

"Ah," Kanako murmured, breaking the silence. "I just thought of something. That detective, he can solve basically any problem for you, right?" She had broken into a grin, as if having hit on a good idea.

"Probably," Matsui answered, not really sure what she was

getting at. "He seemed to suggest as much. He has to be good if they're making movies based on his work."

"Right? And it said that in the trailer, too."

"Is there a mystery you need solving?"

"A mystery . . . I suppose you could call it that. I'm looking for my brother."

Huh? Matsui tilted his head slightly.

Back when she had offered Mitsuki and him glasses of her loquat wine, she had explained that it was her brother who had first started making it. He had even caught her looking at his photo on the cupboard, of the young man who looked just like her. He had assumed from the conversation that he must have died young.

"I don't know where he is."

"I see," he nodded. "Me too," he added cautiously after a moment of thought.

"You too?"

"Yes. I've been searching for someone myself."

"Then why don't we look together? This has to be fate. A taxi driver out looking for someone picks up a great detective as a passenger, and then when you can't find him again, you bump into me, also trying to find someone. It must be a message from God, telling us both to ask the detective for help."

Kanako was good at connecting the dots to find solutions through fragmentary episodes like this. She knew full well that she had quite the knack for finding the hidden links between seemingly unrelated events, which was partly why she had started working at the consultation room in the first place.

"He's a famous detective, with several movies made about him," Kanako continued in her consultant voice. "I'm sure he must have a never-ending stream of clients. Maybe he doesn't usually take on jobs as simple as tracking someone down, but he told you his life story, right? About how he was going to see a movie starring his father? There must have been something between you two for him to start talking about his private life. So maybe he'll be willing to make an exception and take your case?"

"Ah." Matsui raised a hand to get a word in. "Unfortunately, he didn't give me any contact information," he said with a shake of his head. "I gave him my business card, but I didn't get his."

"He must have mentioned something we can use as a clue, though? It doesn't matter what. First things first, Shuro *is* his real name, right? First? Last? He didn't give any other names?"

Matsui turned his mind back to that talk about keys and apartments. "Come to think of it, he said he was constantly moving house, and that he used to be a magician before becoming a detective."

It was the strangest of stories.

The two of them wanted to hire a detective to track down missing family and friends, but before they knew it, they were pooling their wits to locate the detective himself.

"Right. He said he used to go by a different name back then—the Mighty Tashiro."

At that moment, a loud clatter rang through the diner. Matsui, Kanako, and the women all caught their breath, turning to the source of the sound.

It was Ayano.

With trembling fingertips, she reached out to the shattered white plates scattered around her feet, succeeding only in smearing them all with red.

1:00 A.M. rolled around once more.

In the prop warehouse at the film studio, Mitsuki bowed her head to Maeda, the warehouse manager.

"I'm sorry. I'm finished now," she said softly.

"Did you find—*szoo*—anything good?" With the gap in his front teeth, a low whistling sound rang out whenever Maeda spoke.

"No," Mitsuki answered.

"Ah. *Szoo*. A shame."

"I really am sorry. It isn't easy sourcing certain items after hours . . ."

"It's fine. *Szoo*. Just as long as we can make a good film."

A good film? Mitsuki shook her head. *Will some minor prop really make any difference?*

It was a question she had asked herself countless times over the years.

"I'll come back in the morning," she said to the warehouse manager.

"Right. Good work. *Szoo*. Get some rest."

No, not yet. Mitsuki shook her head hastily. *It's too early to call it a day.*

Leaving the warehouse, she noticed the red filming light on the north side of Studio D. She wasn't the only one working late, she reminded herself.

"Exactly. Heck, *I'm* pulling an all-nighter," the assistant director Mizushima griped once she arrived back in the waiting room. "Anyway, Mitsuki. Did you find it?"

"No, I'm afraid not . . . "

"Ah. Well. So, what are you gonna do now? We need it by noon, yeah?"

"I'll figure something out."

"I hope so."

"That's what a procurer does."

Problems like this called for only one person. *Please, please, please, let this one turn out okay,* she prayed as she pulled out her cellphone, dialed Matsui, and closed her eyes.

"Why are you calling *me* for this? Wouldn't it make more sense to ask *him*?" Matsui teased, uncharacteristically buoyant.

"*Him*?"

"Your Crow Professor."

"Ah." Mitsuki's voice dropped an octave.

Concerned, Matsui stole a glance in the rearview mirror. "I'm not sure if it's any of my business, but do you mind if I bring it up . . . ?"

"Hmm?"

"Your ring."

"Ah." Mitsuki's voice dropped again. "It stands out, huh?"

"I wouldn't say that, exactly."

The light ahead turned red. Matsui eased to a stop before the intersection.

"Really, it isn't all that conspicuous," he continued, trying to reassure her. "If anything, it's classy—chic, even. It's just, you seem to be fretting over it."

"I mean, it won't come off."

"Right . . . " Matsui hesitated over his next words. "Do you *want* to take it off?"

The traffic signal turned green, and his midnight-blue taxi slipped quietly onto the national highway.

The area surrounding the film studio was a quiet residential district, devoid of shops or entertainment venues. Since Mitsuki was a regular customer, Matsui was used to navigating the area, but the roads were so sparsely lit that if he didn't check his GPS, he was likely to lose his way.

"So, um, what you're saying is this—you're having a hard time making a decision, I take it?" he asked.

"Eh?"

Mitsuki startled at the word *decision*, but when she stopped to think about it, she realized that Matsui had hit the mark.

"I thought I'd have more time to think about it," she answered softly. "I wasn't ready."

"Ah, I see."

"Hold on. Aren't you married, Matsui?"

"Don't worry about me. But it isn't just marriage, is it? Whenever you have a big decision to make, you always wish you still had more time. Am I right?"

"I suppose that's true," Mitsuki nodded, averting her gaze and staring into the darkness beyond the window. "But it's not just sentimentality," she continued, looking back at him through the rearview mirror. "The ring just won't come off. Physically speaking."

"Ah." Matsui's face clouded over for a moment, before giving way to a faint smile. "So *that's* what you meant. Yes, that sounds a lot like you. You hate to lose."

"It's really getting on my nerves. Not just the idea of marriage. It's like a toy puzzle ring. I won't be able to put it out of mind until I get it off. Honestly, I feel like it's hounding me everywhere I go," she explained, caressing the ring with one finger.

"Sounds like fate," Matsui said, as though hitting on some kind of solution.

"Oh? Is *that* it?" Mitsuki answered with an exaggerated nod. "What about you, Matsui? I'm sorry to keep asking, but do you have a wife, or a partner?"

She leaned forward to see whether there was a ring on the

fingers gripping the steering wheel. Matsui, however, always wore the white gloves that were the hallmark of his trade, so she couldn't tell.

"No, no, don't worry about me," he answered with another shake of his head. "Yes, maybe it *is* fate," he repeated softly, as if the words were meant now for himself.

"Hmm . . . ?"

"By the way, Mitsuki," Matsui spoke up. "Have you ever heard of a Detective Shuro?"

"Huh? How do you know about *Shuro*?"

"You *do* know him?"

"Of course. The props I've been gathering lately—most of them are for the latest *Shuro* project. Why do you ask?"

"Ah . . . " Matsui let out a low murmur.

This was exactly what he had meant by the word *fate*. One night, a humble taxi driver picks up either the lead actor in a film or else the man his character was modelled on (Matsui still couldn't say which), and a few days later, he gets a call from a girl procuring props for the same film.

Naturally, this coincidence had taken him by surprise. At the same time, however, a nihilistic part of him mumbled *Of course*.

As he had told his colleagues many times, Tokyo was considerably smaller than one might think.

In this city, there were all sorts of reasons why people might bump into one another, countless paths and opportunities by which they might connect. Ever since starting in this line of work, he had come to learn that the likelihood of some kind of chance encounter or another was overwhelmingly high.

"No way," he remembered an old friend telling him once. "Tokyo is the biggest city in the whole country. Doesn't that mean you've got the *lowest* chance of bumping into whoever you wanna find?"

Of course, Matsui knew that this conclusion was only logical. However, when you consider that every person has their own connections, that those networks spread out in a myriad of intricate ways, you realize that the greater the number of people, the greater the rate of the spread, like a contagious disease.

"No, no, no," his friend insisted. "Coincidences like that just don't happen. This ain't the countryside. How many times have *you* bumped into someone you know just walking around the city? Not often, I'll bet."

That wasn't true, Matsui knew. Most people just didn't notice it.

People in this city passed each other by in far more places and on far more occasions than they realized.

For instance, they might come within a block of a relative or close acquaintance during some random outing. They just didn't know it.

Even if they were to pass each other at close range on the same street, they would most likely be forever oblivious to that fact. There were simply too many people around, too many other faces in the crowd. But when you narrowed down to a specific situation—say, a taxi—you began to notice just how frequent those coincidences really were.

Matsui himself had picked up the same customer many a time, without any booking. He would be driving around town and happen to pick up a customer hailing the nearest cab, only to discover they were the same customer he had picked up somewhere else a week earlier. It wasn't because of their face or voice that he recognized them, but because they got off at the same apartment building that he recalled from last time.

Plenty of other taxi drivers would give similar testimonies. Interestingly, unless a driver's face or name was particularly distinctive, most customers remained unaware that they had journeyed with the same one.

And so, a part of Matsui always believed that somewhere along the line, *she* would step into his car once again.

"So?" Mitsuki's level voice called out to him. "What about *Shuro*?"

"It's nothing really," Matsui answered softly with a shake of his head. "I just had a customer tell me about the films."

"Ah, right. They're pretty popular, you know?"

"The prop you're looking for tonight, that isn't for a *Detective Shuro* movie, is it?"

"No, not tonight. It's for a different one. They've got me working on two projects at the same time," Mitsuki answered, still playing with the ring on her finger.

She probably didn't even realize, but she was applying considerable force to it.

"What kind of film is it, then?"

"A chick flick."

"What's the title?"

"*Eleven Marias*."

"So, how's the film coming along? Everything going smoothly?" Ayano asked.

"I guess so," Haruka answered with a frown, slowly stirring sugar into her coffee. "It's just, the making-of film crew is always on our backs. There's never a chance to relax."

"Making-of?"

"They're doing a documentary about the film. I think they're planning on using it as a bonus feature or something when it comes out on DVD and the like."

"That's incredible! The movie isn't even out yet!"

"They're probably betting it'll be valuable footage later. You know, of what everything was like before the big debut."

"Right, right."

"Anyway, it's like we're caught in the middle of two separate film shoots. There's the film crew shooting the movie itself, and this special TV documentary about its production."

"Woah. Must make your head spin?"

"Tell me about it."

"You're moving up in the world, Haruka. Leaving us all behind."

"Cut it out."

The two friends had met at a café in the heart of Tokyo, a venue that they had frequented since their university days. It had only taken exchanging a few casual greetings for them both to realize just how exhausted the other looked.

"Has something happened?" Haruka asked bluntly.

"What?" Ayano shot back, clearly upset despite putting on her best effort to keep her cool.

"Come on, don't play dumb," Haruka insisted. "You got in touch because something's up, right? You know better than anyone just how busy I am, but you called me anyway."

"Sorry . . . "

"Look, it's written all over your face. *Something* has happened."

At this, Ayano reflexively raised a hand to her cheek.

"Spit it out. Whatever it is, I'll listen. I'm the oldest of eleven siblings. I'm used to playing older sister."

It was true that Haruka seemed to have grown two sizes, both physically and mentally.

"Alright then," Ayano sighed, catching her breath. "I'm pretty sure I've mentioned him a few times before, but it's Tashiro . . . "

"Huh?" Haruka's eyes, already larger than most, widened still. "You're still hung up on him? You've gotta learn when to move on. Didn't you say he was a magician or something? If you ask me, he sounds more like a con artist."

"I know . . . " Ayano found herself nodding in agreement.

"He's like, like a lizard, you know? What do you call them, those ones that change color?"

"Chameleons?"

"Right, right," Haruka nodded. "Like one of those. Elusive,

you know? I don't know if I should say this, but once—I don't even remember when it was—but I dropped by your old diner for dinner, and he came in while I was eating."

"He's not like that," Ayano interrupted, having heard this story countless times before. "*You* said you wanted to see what kind of guy he was."

"I did? Anyway, he made a pass at me. That's just the kind of guy he is. He's not just dangerous—he's like some kind of hazardous material. But still, go on. What about him?"

"You're not making this easy . . . "

"Sorry, sorry. Forget what I just said."

"Anyway, it was one of the regulars. That taxi driver, Matsui," Ayano said, glancing furtively around the café. "I heard him say he gave Tashiro a ride."

"What do you mean? How do you know it was *that* Tashiro?"

"Well, I don't *know*, not a hundred percent. But Matsui was saying he's an actor, that he used to be a magician called the Mighty Tashiro."

"Ah, right, yeah. I remember you saying he used to go by that stage name. I didn't believe you."

"It's not just that. Matsui said he played the main character in a detective movie that came out a while back. He basically implied he was the detective himself."

"Seriously?"

"That's when it all clicked. I went to Maruya right away. I wasn't even thinking."

"Maruya?"

"A video rental store. It's only a ten minute walk, but even that felt like too long to wait, so I jumped onto my bicycle and pedaled there as fast as I could just to see if it was true. I was in such a rush! When I asked the staff if they had anything called *Detective Shuro*, sure enough, they did."

"Huh? Shuro?"

"You've heard of it?"

"Heard of it? The studio I'm working at now *made* it."

"Oh. Wow . . . "

"So of course I know about it. Wasn't it a big hit? They're working on a whole series for it right now," Haruka explained.

Hearing this, Ayano knew in her bones that her friend really was leaving her behind.

"You can be pretty out of things sometimes, you know?" Haruka said. "You do realize I work for one of Japan's biggest film companies, right?"

Ayano sank deep into the mire of her own thoughts.

What on earth am I doing?

Both Tashiro and Haruka were somehow working for some huge company—a film studio, at that. No, hold on. Tashiro wasn't *in* the movie, per se. The main character was simply based on him.

"But they were so similar. The detective—Shuro—and Tashiro, I mean," Ayano said, excited.

"Hey, calm down," Haruka cautioned her with a stern look. "It's a movie, right? Just because they look similar doesn't mean Tashiro is actually that detective, does it?"

"But they're *so* similar. I'm sure of it. I heard Matsui say he didn't know whether he was the actor or the detective, but *I* knew at once. The actor *did* look like him, but he wasn't Tashiro himself. So he *must* have become a detective. A real detective. And a famous one at that."

"Huh? Can you say that again?" Matsui murmured.

Mitsuki licked her chapped lips. "A peanut sheller," she enunciated clearly.

"A sheller?" Matsui repeated. "For peanuts? I thought they were for walnuts?"

"Exactly. Weird, don't you think? And he wanted something a little older. It seems like it's a particularly important prop."

"Hmm . . . " Matsui's voice trailed off when he hit on an idea.

When was it, exactly? He had been driving down a back road after dropping a client off in Shimokitazawa, and he had spotted a store with the lights still on. That sight had been unusual enough for him to slow down to take a closer look, only to find it was an antiques shop. *At this time of night?* he remembered thinking as he checked his watch. After all, it was 3:00 A.M.

"Take me there," Mitsuki requested.

"Very well. I hope I can find it again . . . "

The moonlight kept close watch on the night-colored taxi as it made its way across the city.

"Hmm. I see," Ibaragi murmured softly to himself.

He had been watching the moon for some time now, and he still wasn't tired of looking at it. In his right hand, he held a long, thin, silver cylinder, while with his left he adjusted a dial, splitting the moon into two within the eyepiece.

"I love this thing."

He had long forgotten where he found the telescope. He had no idea what it even was back when he had first purchased it, but his gut intuition told him that it was the perfect item for his store.

Thinking up an elaborate name for the shop had been too much trouble, so he had simply written his surname, Ibaragi, on the signboard with the intention of opening a perfectly ordinary antiques shop. But all shops ultimately reflected their owners' personalities, so in the end, the store Ibaragi turned into a veritable house of curiosities.

To begin with, he observed opposite hours to most people. He would open the doors at nine in the evening, and lock them again at around four in the morning, just as he was beginning to grow drowsy and dawn began to break.

And Ibaragi was a drowsy sort.

He was averse to the noonday sun, and would often scurry

off to some dimly lit place to catch some shuteye. He had been that way ever since he was a child. *Bat syndrome*, he liked to call it. Thinking up clever names for things was another part of his job.

"A moonlight amplifier," he mumbled, conjuring up a name for the cylindrical object.

Now that he knew what to call the mysterious piece of junk, all that remained was to write it down on a tag and give it an appropriate price.

To the uninitiated, the item might have seemed like no more than a broken telescope. Ibaragi, however, was always happy to see broken goods put to new uses.

When manmade objects were broken, they were reborn as something else. So went his pet theory.

Whenever something created for a specific purpose wore down—and this was true of most tools that humans built—it was liberated from its human-imposed application. Only then was it set free.

That was how he saw it.

His work, his calling, was to find the true names for those items freed from their former roles.

In short, almost everything in his store was broken.

He had everything—invisible ink pens, half hats, hot-air machine guns, water temperers, and more.

The store was filled from floor to ceiling with oddly named items, but in part because the merchandise was all broken and in part because of his odd operating hours, the number of customers who dropped by had been steadily dwindling.

Satisfied that he had come up with a suitable name for his newest product, Ibaragi stepped back inside from the alleyway and sat down at his work desk. He opened his book, as per his usual routine, secure in the belief that he was unlikely to have any more customers for the rest of the night.

The only thing left was to read until he fell asleep.

At that moment, however, the front door clattered open. Looking up with a squint, he spotted two figures standing in the entranceway.

It was a man and a woman. Not a couple, if appearances were any indication. He could tell at once that there was a noticeable age gap between them, but they didn't quite strike him as father and daughter, either.

Well then.

It took him a moment to notice in the dim light, but the man was wearing what looked like a taxi driver uniform.

It wasn't Ibaragi's job to judge, but he had heard about strange enterprises like this—taxi companies whose usage numbers had plummeted, turning instead to running late-night sightseeing tours throughout the city. The idea was to take clients to late-night parks, late-night stadiums, late-night restaurants, and late-night stores so they could experience firsthand Tokyo's lesser-known nocturnal side.

If he had to guess at the identities of the good-natured taxi driver and the young woman who seemed oddly tired of life, it would have to be that. Still, he would never have expected his store to be selected as one of those destinations.

Ibaragi nodded to himself, convinced of his assessment.

Meanwhile, Matsui and Mitsuki, unaware that they had been so thoroughly misappraised, stood transfixed by the miscellaneous, elaborately labeled items occupying the store shelves.

"Hello?" Mitsuki called out hesitatingly.

"Yes? Can I help you?" Ibaragi replied, surprised by the brightness of her voice.

Ibaragi had guessed that Mitsuki was tired of life, but it seemed she might simply be exhausted from a long day's work.

"Actually, I'm looking for something," she ventured.

"I see," he replied cautiously, before launching into the same advisory he gave any customer who came in looking for any specific item. "I say this to all my customers because I don't want you to leave disappointed. Rather than helping you find what you're looking for, in this store, things usually go smoother when you find what you're looking for yourself . . . This is your first time in a shop like this, isn't it?"

"I understand," Mitsuki answered quickly. "I think I'd have a great time here if it wasn't for work."

"Work?"

"Yes. I'm looking for a prop for a movie."

Mitsuki was beginning to wonder whether she hadn't fallen asleep in the back seat of Matsui's taxi. Her mind was still at full throttle, which might explain why she was having such a bizarre dream.

After all, what kind of antiques store was open in the middle of the night?

"What are you looking for?" Ibaragi asked, uttering a phrase that seldom left his lips. "Maybe I can help you."

"Well. It's for peanuts. You know how they come in shells?"

"Yes, of course."

"I'm looking for something that can crush them, I think. A peanut sheller? Like what you use for walnuts."

"Ah. A peanut crusher," Ibaragi said as if it was the most natural thing in the world.

"You have one?" Mitsuki cried out.

"We do. Large, medium, and small ones. What size do you need?"

T he hands on Moriizumi's watch pointed to 1:00 A.M.
If she didn't wind it, it would soon start lagging by five
minutes or more. By all metrics, the worn-out device
was ready to be thrown in the trash, but Moriizumi couldn't
bring herself to replace it.

Not that there was any good reason behind her attachment
to it. If there was, she would be able to overturn it with some
kind of logical counterargument. But when there was no ratio-
nal reason why she shouldn't let go of it in the first place, the
situation wasn't quite so easy.

Checking the address on her map one last time, she rang the
doorbell outside her client's apartment at exactly one o'clock in
the morning.

She couldn't afford to knock at the wrong door at this time
of night.

Funnily enough, ever since she had started advertising that
she could arrange collections even in the middle of the night,
the majority of orders that came through were from people who
preferred a late-night pickup.

That being said, such requests were extremely rare from female clients.

Moriizumi stood warily at the door as she heard someone
approach, pause for a short moment, then unlock the door
with a loud click. She had told the client—a Ms. Fukuda—over
the phone that she would make the pickup in person, and her
cheerful *I'm glad to hear that* still rang fresh in her ears.

"Ah, you're here!" came that same light voice as Fukuda opened the door ten centimeters to peer back at her through the darkness. Those ten centimeters gradually stretched to thirty, until at last she was invited inside.

Several pairs of plain high heels and leather shoes were neatly lined up in the entranceway. Even before stepping inside, Moriizumi, through long experience, had already guessed her client's personality—serious, neat, and likely somewhat introverted.

Broadly speaking, there were two kinds of people when it came to telephone disposal pickups.

The first were those who hated telephones and telecommunication systems as a whole. They practically burned with animosity for the devices. *Just take it. Do whatever you want with the thing.*

The other group was the exact opposite—those who had a strong attachment to their telephones. They all had their own reasons, but one of the most common was that they had recently started using a PC or a cellphone after a lifetime communicating with loved ones over the landline. After all that time, they had ended up developing an almost fetishistic attachment to the devices themselves.

Moriizumi's first impression of Emi Fukuda was that she too was bound by memory to her old telephone. Unable to discard it herself, no doubt she had hesitated for a time before ultimately calling a collection agency to do it for her. She appeared to be relatively young, but watching her under the fluorescent light as she pointed to a corner of the room, Moriizumi couldn't help but notice that she looked worn, tired, like someone who had accumulated a lifetime of experience.

"Here it is," Fukuda said, her hands placed tenderly atop the telephone.

In cases like this, Moriizumi knew that it was best to follow the client's lead. Some would scream at the top of their lungs if she was too rough pulling the wires out of the wall, while others would refuse to let her collect the device at all, claiming to have changed their minds.

As such, she put on a pair of white gloves, carefully removed the telephone as though handling a precious jewel, and delicately placed it in the cloth bag she had brought with her.

"That concludes the collection," she said solemnly, using language hewing close to what was used at her family's funeral home.

Emi Fukuda, perhaps impressed by this show of reverence, stopped her on her way out. "Um, if you don't mind . . . maybe you could stay for tea?"

If she had been her usual self, Moriizumi would have responded simply *No, that's alright, thank you,* and been on her way.

But Fukuda seemed to be pleading with her. *"Stay just a little longer."*

Moriizumi couldn't resist. "Just a quick drink," she said, making a special exception.

Strictly speaking, she was curious about those last words, *Stay just a little longer.*

Was Emi Fukuda saying she wanted to stay by the telephone for a few more minutes? Or was she asking that Moriizumi herself stay?

It was a cozy studio apartment, with a kitchenette to the side and an electric kotatsu, the only thing even resembling a table, installed in the center of the room. The only other items of note were a small closet, a bookshelf, and a wardrobe.

Moriizumi sat by the kotatsu as she removed her gloves. "You won't be using the landline anymore?" she asked, her standard question.

"No. I've been making do with my cellphone for a while now," came the standard response.

The reason Moriizumi was kept so busy in recent years was because there was no end to the number of people who no longer needed a landline. Those who continued to hold onto them despite the march of technological progress largely did so because they wanted to keep their old numbers.

For instance, suppose you had interacted with someone before you started using a cellphone. Those contacts would only know your fixed telephone number, and even though you weren't in touch with them right now, there was no telling if you would receive a call sometime in the future.

There were plenty of people in that boat. After all, if they discarded their old number, they would risk severing the threads tying them to those old contacts forever.

Moriizumi couldn't say for sure, but she suspected that Emi Fukuda belonged to that category.

All the same, she didn't want to ask any nosy questions. She didn't need to ask to listen, and she already had a pretty good idea of what was going on. Besides, as clumsy as she was, she doubted that she would be able to come out with anything tactful.

Moriizumi made a point never to ask a client about their individual circumstances, but that wouldn't stop them from broaching the topic themselves. This was especially likely to happen after any offer of tea or the like.

Half resigned to those conversations, she would nod along no matter the subject, keeping her own emotions in check while responding with simple platitudes like *That must be tough*.

And yet, when Emi Fukuda offered her a cup of tea, what she said was: "You see, there's a bat on the veranda."

"Huh?" Moriizumi asked back. "Did you say a *bat*?"

"Yes," Emi Fukuda nodded, indicating to the curtains at the end of the room. "Over there."

In other words, the veranda behind the curtains.

Not sure how to respond, Moriizumi stared at the curtains until the long silence grew too oppressive to bear.

"That must be tough," came her prepared response.

"It's there right now."

Emi Fukuda kept her back ramrod straight as she stared at the curtains. She was acting as though her eyes could see right through the fabric to the balcony beyond, her gaze so fervent that even Moriizumi began to imagine the creature's faint outline.

The bat was sleeping under the eaves of the veranda, hanging upside down in its customary position. Or maybe it was only pretending to be asleep, secretly watching the woman's movements inside the room? If it had been a European balcony from another age, the creature might have been considered a servant or incarnation of a vampire, its presence enough to make any young woman tremble in fear.

Perhaps Moriizumi was imagining things, but when Emi Fukuda had uttered the word *bat*, the corners of her eyes had seemed to slant downward slightly. If anything, it seemed like maybe she was eagerly anticipating the bat's arrival, waiting for it to transform into a beautiful young man dressed entirely in black.

That youth would linger on the veranda behind the curtain, unable to bring himself to speak up but hoping desperately to be reunited with the woman inside.

The woman wasn't without hope of her own. Her reluctance to part with her old telephone number was proof enough of that. Deep in her heart of hearts, she had been passing the years waiting for the man's return.

And at long last, here he was.

After an eternity following his only clue—the telephone wire—from utility pole to utility pole throughout the labyrinthine city, finally he had arrived at this very balcony.

But he was too late.

The woman, weary of waiting, had decided to sever the weak thread connecting the two of them, calling the number of a telephone collection company listed on a flyer that appeared one day in her mailbox.

And so the man was left dangling, his fate up in the air.

He became a bat.

Somehow, he had managed to reach the boundary line—the veranda outside her apartment—but already the barriers were in place. The telephone line had been disconnected, and all hope was lost.

At that point, Moriizumi shook her head to clear away the unruly fantasy.

"Are you really sure about this?" she asked, checking one last time.

"Yes." Emi Fukuda nodded. "It's been long enough."

With that, the room descended into silence once more.

Just as Moriizumi was about to take her leave, Emi Fukuda spoke up: "I . . . I work at a department store."

"Oh?" Moriizumi, halfway to her feet, returned to her seat. "Are you a sales clerk?"

"No. I'm an elevator girl."

"Ah." She couldn't think of anything else to say. *So what?* she wanted to add, but stopped herself.

"I'm thinking of quitting."

"Oh?"

"For every elevator girl, there comes a time when you need to call it quits."

"Ah," Moriizumi said once more. *Right, there's probably an age limit or something. They do call them* girls, *after all.*

"It isn't because of my age."

"Ah. I see," Moriizumi answered, now at a total loss.

"The hat won't suit me much longer."

"The hat?"

"Nothing is more important to an elevator girl than her hat. Even if she's having a bad makeup day, or her smile isn't what it once was, she still looks good so long as she wears the hat. Without it, no one would think of me as an elevator girl."

"They wouldn't?"

"*He* wouldn't either . . . "

Was it a coincidence that Emi Fukuda stole a glance at the veranda while murmuring those words?

"He always complimented my hat."

"This man—he's someone important to you?" Moriizumi asked.

"Yes. He called me sometimes."

I knew it. She almost broke into a laugh to hear that her wild fantasy hadn't been totally off the mark, but she held her tongue. This kind of thing wasn't entirely uncommon in the funeral business, either, and it was never appropriate to laugh.

"He was an elderly gentleman."

Ah, I see.

"He passed away."

Ah. That explains it.

"But even though he passed, he still called me from time to time."

Huh?

Moriizumi felt a chill run down her spine. *People really do know how to give you a fright, huh?*

Her usual rejoinder—*That must be tough*—was hardly appropriate here, but she didn't know what else to say. Her best option, she calmly decided, was to leave as quickly as possible while keeping any further conversation to a minimum.

"I should be off. I have another pickup," she said, rising to her feet with the telephone in its cloth bag and hurrying back to the front door, taking pains not to look back either to the curtain or to Emi Fukuda's face.

As she slipped on her shoes and reached for the doorknob, a presence suddenly loomed behind her.

"Your money."

She glanced over her shoulder to see Emi Fukuda standing right behind her, holding out a strangely pale envelope.

"Thank you."

Moriizumi wanted to snatch the envelope out of her hands

and run away as fast as her feet would carry her, but she forced herself to respond with a casual smile as she stepped out the doorway.

Don't look back. Go straight to the car. Luckily—hold on, luckily? Anyway, I should have some mourning clothes from the funeral home in the car. There should be some purifying salt in one of the pockets. Let's just spread some around and forget this whole thing ever happened.

The telephone in the cloth bag felt suddenly cold and heavy.

"Are you really happy with that?" Matsui asked Mitsuki before starting the car, just to be sure.

Her response was entirely as he had expected. "I'm not sure," she murmured under her breath. "To be honest, I don't have the faintest clue what the director had in mind. Maybe even he doesn't know. I mean, *is* there such a thing as a peanut sheller?"

"Hmm. To me, that looks like a normal set of needle-nose pliers."

"I know," Mitsuki nodded in agreement. "I thought so too. I mean, that's *definitely* what they are. But the man in the store—"

"Yes, he was very upfront about it. I can't remember how many times he pointed out that he's the only one who actually calls it a *peanut crusher*."

"Yes, it's like I can still hear him. He had a very unusual way of talking, didn't he?"

"*Society at large might call it something else, just so you know,*" Matsui said, giving his best impression of the store owner.

"Yes," Mitsuki nodded again, as if responding to the man himself. "The rest of the world might call it something else, but if *someone* calls it a peanut crusher, then that's what it is."

"Let's hope so," Matsui agreed. "If no one has ever seen the real thing before, who's to say if it is or isn't?"

"Yes, that's right. " Mitsuki mumbled.

Indeed, so long as no one was expecting to see something

else, they couldn't possibly complain. Then again, Matsui considered, maybe he alone had never heard of a peanut sheller, and the rest of the world was well aware of what they were. There were countless things like that in life.

For instance, even if Mitsuki had no idea what a peanut crusher looked like, she must still have been able to recognize the man popularly known as Detective Shuro.

"Um," he began, summoning up the courage to ask her. "Sorry about changing the subject, but can you tell me what this Detective Shuro fellow looks like?"

"What he looks like?" Mitsuki blinked in surprise. "Which one do you mean?" she asked, pulling out her cellphone.

"Well . . . " This time, it was Matsui's turn to let his gaze wander. "How about the man playing him in the film?"

Mitsuki searched online for an image of the actor playing the movie Shuro, pinching to enlarge it before showing it to Matsui.

"He's a newcomer," she explained. "He got the role at the audition because the producers wanted someone who looked as close to the real Shuro as possible. What was his name again . . . ? Ah, right. Tetsuo Serikawa. I think this is the only film he's been in so far."

No sooner did he lay eyes on the photo than Matsui shook his head. "That wasn't him," he replied, pursing his lips.

Mitsuki searched online once again, this time bringing up an image of the real Shuro. "How about this one, then?"

Matsui stared into the screen, mentally comparing the image to the face he remembered in the rearview mirror. "Ah, that's him, alright. No doubt about it."

"Hmm . . . "

Kanako Fuyuki stared at the computer display, slowly examining each of the images of *Detective Shuro* that came up in the search results.

"Not bad, huh? They're both pretty good looking," she murmured, looking back and forth between the actor and the man himself.

Yes, her curiosity had indeed been piqued.

Shinichi Goto, at the desk beside her, peered up at the display, his eyes cold. "What are you mumbling about, Kanako? I won't stop you if you want to look up photos of handsome guys, but I'm going home. Can you take over?"

"Yeah, yeah." Kanako was in an unusually good mood tonight.

Moving from her private desk to her usual position at desk twenty-five, she set herself up with a small bottle of mineral water, her cellphone, her glasses, a notepad, and a ballpoint pen, and then fitted the headset.

"Let's get started," she called out into the Tokyo night.

Though she wasn't addressing anyone in particular, calls soon started coming in one after the other. If she were in sales, she thought with a smile, she would no doubt be raking it in.

Kanako, however, received a fixed salary regardless of the number of calls she received or the amount of time she spent on the phone. As such, she wouldn't have any opportunities to boast about how many calls she might take in a single night. All the same, that night, each call was relatively short—simple problems that could be resolved in just a couple of minutes—and so she set a new personal record.

For instance, one caller wanted to know where they could buy watercolors in the middle of the night, a problem with an immediate solution.

When it came to complex cases, it was often difficult to understand a caller's problem at first, to figure out what they were worrying about, why there were suffering, or what had plunged them into depression.

On this particular day, however, she simply had to give the standard advice on career paths and getting over a broken heart—and so Kanako, already in a good mood, kept on talking nonstop for a full two hours.

Just as her energy was waning and she was considering taking a break to grab a canned coffee, she heard a woman crying over the line.

"Tokyo No. 3 Consultation Room, how can I help?" she asked.

She won't stop crying.

"Are you okay?"

"Sorry," came a loud sniffle as the caller blew her nose on a seemingly endless stream of tissues.

"There's no need to rush. Take your time," Kanako told both the woman and herself in the calmest voice she could muster. "What should I call you? It doesn't have to be your real name."

"Eiko," came a subdued voice a moment later.

Kanako scribbled the name down as *A-ko* on her notepad, though she did consider picking out a set of kanji characters to give her a real name, something like *splendor child*, perhaps. Given how quickly the woman had answered, Kanako suspected it was her real name.

A lot of callers liked to adopt a pseudonym like B or Sally, so they could tell themselves for a moment that their problems belonged to someone else. That being said, since they weren't meeting face-to-face and this would be a one-off encounter between caller and consultant, there was nothing wrong with giving a real name, either.

"Things aren't going well," A-ko said after a long pause. Then, in a whisper, she added: "But I have to pretend like they are."

Kanako still didn't know the specifics, but this was a common enough beginning for a consultation session. She had heard the same thing many times before. In any relationship, be it between parent and child, lovers, or even committed couples, there often came a time when one party would say *I'm sick of pretending.*

"With whom?" Kanako asked softly. "Who are you having trouble with?"

"Everyone."

"Everyone?"

"It isn't working out with anyone."

"And how many people are we talking about here?"

"There's eleven of us. All girls."

All girls?

The caller seemed to be settling down, but Kanako still couldn't guess how old she was, what with her constant crying. But she had said *girls*, so that probably made her a young woman.

Kanako pondered her next question for a moment, then asked frankly: "What kind of girls?"

"We were chosen," the caller answered.

Huh?

Kanako rested a finger on her chin. It was by no means rare, having a caller claiming to be *chosen* in some way and wondering why they couldn't make life work. On closer inspection, however, that tended to be no more than their own self-evaluation. In most cases, they hadn't really been chosen for anything.

"What were you chosen for?" she asked.

"In an audition. For a movie."

At this response, Kanako placed her hands on the desk and straightened her back. "So you're an actress?"

"No, this was my first audition. Some of the other girls have worked in other films before, though. Um, maybe that's why it isn't going well? Because of the difference in *commitment*, you know?"

Huh? She's sharper than I thought.

Kanako hastily changed the triangle mark that she had scribbled on her notepad to a circle. She used a circle when a caller made their point clearly, a triangle for average conversations, and a cross when she just couldn't make heads or tails of it.

Kanako began putting the pieces in order. "So basically, eleven girls, yourself included, auditioned for a movie, and you all got roles. And now, the eleven of you aren't getting along?"

"That's right."

"But you need to *pretend* like everything is going smoothly."

"Not just me. We all have to."

"When was the audition?"

"Around a month ago."

"And what are you doing now? Have you started filming?"

"No, we're doing workshops to prepare for the shoot."

"And that's what isn't going well?"

"No, not that. Things are fine during the workshops, but when we go back to the dormitory—"

"Dormitory? You're staying in a dormitory?"

"Yes. We're all living together . . . "

So that's it.

Kanako quickly jotted down what she had just heard. This was by no means a *simple* case, but at the same time, she had a decent grasp of what was going on now.

"What is the dormitory like?" she asked. "Are you there now?"

"Yes."

"Can anyone hear you, by any chance?"

"No, we're in separate rooms."

"One room per person?"

"Yes. Most of the girls are from towns in the countryside."

I see, I see. It's all coming together now, Kanako nodded as she took notes.

"You're all girls. There aren't any adults there, I take it?"

"Um, there's the housemother."

"Anyone else?"

"No."

"No leader or captain in the group?"

"Nothing like that. They told us everyone's an equal here."

"Who said that?"

"The director, the producers, the mangers . . . All the adults on the set."

"The set?"

"The studio, I mean. We're supposed to start filming in two weeks, so we're spending every day between the dormitory and the set . . . But I'm afraid some of the girls will end up quitting at this rate . . . And I don't think I can keep going, either."

"I see." Kanako crossed her arms and read over her notes from the beginning. "You said there was a housemother, right?"

"She cooks and cleans for us."

"Ah. So you all eat together?"

"Yes. There's a dining room. We all eat there."

That's it, Kanako thought with a flash of realization. "I take it you all eat at the same table?"

"That's right."

"In that case, why not talk things over with everyone after dinner?"

"Everyone goes back to their rooms after eating, though."

"Maybe you can tell them you want to talk and ask them to stay back for a few minutes?"

"I can't. Some of them are older than me. Besides, they're all so independent, and they all see each other as rivals."

"But it's best to discuss this with them," Kanako insisted. "It sounds like there's no clear leader, so unless someone takes the initiative, you won't be able to come together as a group."

"I see . . . "

"Why don't you give it a try?"

That was her only piece of advice. With eleven girls all wrapped up in their own thoughts and emotions, *nothing* would ever happen unless someone spoke up.

"I understand," A-ko answered after a long silence.

Thank goodness for that, Kanako thought, relieved that she would finally be able to end the call. Nothing had been re-solved, so she wasn't able to come away from the conversation truly relaxed.

Such was her dilemma. Should she really accept this small, temporary sense of relief while the issue remained unsettled?

"Is this really okay?" she wondered aloud—only for the voice of the next client to sound in her ears.

The hour hand reached 1:00 A.M.

"Oh, Eiko?" called a figure in front of the bathroom.

Approaching carefully, Eiko was relieved to see that it was just Haruka—the only other girl in the group she could talk to openly.

Haruka was the oldest of the eleven, but—and Eiko meant this in a positive way—she didn't come across as such. She was always polite to the others and was always the first to take the initiative whenever something came up that the other girls wanted to avoid.

Cleaning the bathroom was one such example. The task *should* have been assigned to each of them in turn, but somewhere along the line, Haruka had ended up taking over responsibility for it.

Eiko had assumed that the housemother was seeing to the cleaning around the dormitory, but after learning that the older woman was living with a long-term back and leg injury, Haruka had suggested that the girls should see to it themselves.

Eiko had learned all this around a fortnight ago, and ever since, she made a point of checking on the bathroom every now and then. Whenever she found Haruka cleaning alone, she stepped in with a helping hand.

"You don't have to," Haruka told her. "Besides, you have an early start tomorrow."

"Why don't we set up a roster for cleaning duties?" Eiko suggested.

"Because some of the girls will say they don't use the bathtub. And it isn't really fair to ask them to clean it if they weren't the ones who used it."

"I guess . . . "

But at the same time, that didn't mean Haruka had to carry this burden alone.

Then again, she seemed willing to take on that responsibility herself if it meant keeping the peace.

Haruka wasn't very good at dealing with conflict, and it hurt her to the core whenever any of the girls quarreled.

But being responsible for cleaning the bathroom did have its own secret advantages. After scrubbing the filth from the bathtub and filling it with fresh hot water, she could enjoy a long relaxing soak without having to worry that the others had used it before her. And since she saw to the cleaning each and every night, she was easily entitled to that small reward.

"Do you think it's okay?" Haruka asked her in private one night.

"Of course," Eiko answered with not a little indignation. "No one has any right to complain. They're always leaving such a mess."

Though they all usually took great care with their appearance and manners, for some reason, they lacked a strong sense of hygiene in the bathroom.

This was due to the fact that many of the girls, not content with the showers in their bedrooms and wanting instead to soak in the large communal bathtub, were somewhat rough around the edges. Every day, the bathroom floor would be splattered with bubbles from various soaps and shampoos, while the room would be littered with empty conditioner packets and boxes of bath salts.

Of course, not everyone was responsible for this mess. At least some girls preferred using their private showers—though Eiko couldn't be sure how many of them there were—and *they* were no doubt a little tidier.

Eiko and Haruka were essentially members of that latter group, but they did enjoy taking a dip in the bathtub every now and then to stretch their legs and have a nice, warm soak.

"Why don't you use the bath once I've finished in here?" Haruka asked. "I'm going to take a shower in my room, but I can fill the tub with fresh water, if you like."

"You're sure? It won't be a problem, me taking it all for myself?"

"Come on, it's fine. There aren't any rules about when you can and can't take a bath. Besides, with the early start tomorrow, everyone seems to have already finished up in here. They've probably all gone to bed."

Maybe I will take the plunge, then, Eiko thought.

But while it would give her an opportunity to stretch her legs and relax, in truth, the bathtub wasn't all that big. Yes, there was sufficient space that a woman could bathe alone and not feel cramped, but it certainly wasn't roomy enough for two.

For that reason, would-be bathers decided who would go first through a game of rock-paper-scissors, taking turns one by one.

Eiko found all this rather tedious, and so had spent the past fortnight without using the bath herself.

"If you insist," she said, accepting Haruka's offer.

"Of course. Can you just do the last bit of cleaning once you're finished?"

"Alright."

"Thanks. See you tomorrow, then."

"Good night."

Eiko listened to Haruka's footsteps as she went from the changing room to the hallway, and once she couldn't hear them anymore, she stuck her head outside to make sure she was alone.

The lights had been switched off, the only source of illumination the dim green blur of the emergency exit sign at the end of the hallway.

The second floor, where the bathroom was located, also housed the dining room, the housemother's room, and a practice room. The housemother, however, went home for one day a week, and on those occasions, the second floor was deserted.

No sounds or voices reached Eiko's ears from the other floors. The entire dormitory seemed quieter than usual.

If anyone happened to notice activity in the bathroom at this late hour, no doubt they would put it down to Haruka cleaning up, and leave it at that.

With that liberating thought, Eiko undressed, took a shower, and for the first time in what felt like forever, sank up to her neck in the rectangular bathtub. The temperature was perfect—and once more, she felt an upswelling of respect for Haruka's keen domestic abilities.

Breathing a heavy sigh, she stared up at the ceiling.

She had passed the audition, and now found herself living under the same roof as the other girls. She was in a privileged position, she reminded herself. Each girl had her own living quarters (albeit a small studio room), and got to eat three meals a day in the spacious dining room (though the eating times were fixed).

Complain, and you'll bring the wrath of the gods down on your head, her grandmother used to say back in her hometown.

Eiko closed her eyes.

Her grandmother had passed away a month ago at a university hospital several dozen kilometers from the family home. Unlike Eiko, who was shy and introverted, her grandmother had always been flamboyant and strong-willed.

Eiko found herself looking back to one of their last conversations. The two of them had been making gyoza dumplings in the kitchen just before she passed her audition and moved to Tokyo.

"This is for your ears only," her grandmother confessed in a hushed voice. "I always wanted to be an actress when I was young."

It wasn't long after Eiko left for Tokyo that her grandmother began to complain of health problems. "She doesn't have much time left," her mother called to tell her one day, holding back her tears. Eiko wanted to hurry home immediately, but faced with her overcrowded schedule, she simply couldn't find the time.

She didn't get to see her grandmother during her final days. In the end, her mother gave her a detailed account of her passing over the phone, but it all felt so unreal. One thing left a strong impression on her, though. The day before she drew her final breath, her grandmother suddenly said: "How I wish I had a cola." Her request was never granted, as she soon slipped into a coma, but someone was considerate enough to run to the convenience store to get a bottle to leave on her pillow.

"Was cola always such a dark color?" her mother asked in a low voice.

"So, that's that, then," Maeda said with a deliberately forlorn expression, no doubt his way of expressing sympathy for Mitsuki's predicament.

Then . . . "*Szoo,*" came the distinctive whistling sound through the gap between his font teeth.

"It's no good? The director actually said that?" she asked, just to be sure.

"Yes. It's just a pair of pliers, he said. I can't exactly say he's wrong on that count." Maeda must have taken her last response as permission to unwind, as he let out a weak chuckle. "What did he call it again, that thing he wants?"

"A peanut crusher."

"Right. Well, that. *Szoo.* You think it really exists?"

"Apparently. The director even drew a picture of it. He said he used it in a shoot decades ago, while still an assistant director. He thought we should still have it in the warehouse. I even checked the film he mentioned in the screening room."

"Did you find it, then?"

"No. I watched the whole movie, but I couldn't see anything like what he mentioned."

"Maybe he just dreamed it up? I wouldn't put it past our good old director."

"Yes, I think he might have . . . "

"But this *is* a problem."

"Yes . . . "

"Times like this call for a drink, Mitsuki."

With those words, Maeda retreated deeper into the warehouse office. Mitsuki couldn't fail to make out the sound of a refrigerator door opening and closing. *Since when did we have a fridge?* she wondered as Maeda came back with a glass in his hand.

The glass was so cold that it had turned white with condensation. It was completely empty, though Mitsuki's imagination had already picked up the aroma of some sweet beverage.

"Look here," Maeda said, straightening his posture. "I used to be a bartender in Ginza, a long time back."

"Oh? I had no idea."

"I got head-hunted. *Szoo.* By these guys."

By these guys—he must have been referring to the film studio.

"Not as an actor, mind you," he added with a wry smile. "This was probably before your time, but there used to be a lounge next to the cafeteria, complete with a bar counter in the corner. Ah, those were the days. Never a dull night. *Szoo.* We made a tidy profit, I'll tell you that. Everyone would thank yours truly that they didn't have to go all the way to Ginza to unwind."

"I see . . . "

"So, back then, the most popular drinks were highballs—both regular ones and others mixed with cola. I could never make anything too complicated, mind you . . . "

"Cola highballs? They've been out of fashion for a while, haven't they? Like a Whiskey and Coke, you mean?"

"Heh. Well, it sounds like a kid's drink, when you say it like that. But if you ask me—*szoo*—there's no beverage easier to whip up, or more delightful, than a good old Whiskey and Coke."

Maeda's use of the word *beverage* rather than *drink*, the way his voice became increasingly polite as he went on, was enough to convince Mitsuki that he was telling the truth. Before she realized it, she found herself licking her lips.

"Do you want to try one?" he asked, making his way back to the refrigerator and returning with a whiskey-filled glass decanter and a regular bottle of cola, both chilled to the cusp of freezing.

"This is our little secret," he said, clearing the service window desk to serve as a makeshift bar counter. "I keep these here for when I need to de-stress."

The recipe was surprisingly simple. Maeda filled a chilled glass with ice cubes, stirring them with a muddler, sans liquid. After making sure that the glass was cold enough to cut your lips, he dumped the ice and poured in a thick layer of freezing whiskey, followed by an equal part cola, quickly mixing them together.

"And presto," Maeda announced, still every bit the bartender.

To be perfectly honest, however, Mitsuki wasn't a strong drinker. Half a beer was usually enough to leave her red-faced and tipsy.

In that state, she would become unusually talkative, breaking out into laughter for the stupidest of reasons. By the end of it, her face would turn deathly pale, and she would end up gasping for air if she didn't find somewhere to lie down. As such, she had to be incredibly careful around alcohol.

Listening to Maeda's story, however, something told her that if she didn't try this Whiskey and Coke, she would regret it for the rest of her life.

No sooner did she take her first sip than her hunch turned to surety—all at once, she rued that her life's journey had kept her from this wonderful *beverage* for so many years, and she was overcome with gratitude for this chance discovery. She was positively ecstatic at the thought of trying it again and again in the days to come.

"Delicious."

It was rare that she spoke that word, but it was the only term capable of conveying the inexpressible feeling that had just come over her.

It was at that moment she recalled a piece of wisdom famous in the film industry: *Don't be too quick to use the word* beautiful.

The word *beautiful* was a symbol, one that denied a person the chance to experience true feeling. It was too utilitarian, too featureless, swallowing up one's every thought, one's impressions, one's sensations, rendering the most important elements devoid of meaning.

As such, those in the art world had grown up being constantly warned by their predecessors not to carelessly utter such all-encompassing words or phrases.

In Mitsuki's experience, however, there were certain things that belied description, for which any verbal account, no matter how clever or witty, served only to diminish, to reduce ineffable splendor to a base, practically vulgar level.

At such times, she was happy to ignore the advice of those who had come before her, and could describe, with full sincerity, a flower or someone's countenance as *beautiful*.

It was with that sentiment that the word *delicious* spilled from her lips.

"It's so delicious it's making my head spin," she whispered softly.

"Right?" Maeda nodded in satisfaction, before preparing another glass for himself.

After bringing it to his lips, he tilted his head to one side, as if to say *Hold on*.

"Heh," he added with a nod. "It *does* leave you feeling a little lightheaded."

"It's like the whole world is spinning around and around . . . "

Eiko wondered which came first, the tremor that shook her body from the tailbone up, or the uniform rippling of the water's surface.

"What?" she wondered aloud, sitting up and staring at the ceiling, then looking down again at the surface of the bathwater.

It was most definitely rippling.

The next moment, the entire bathtub seemed to bounce, and the unusual sideways, rolling vibrations began in earnest.

For a long second, she had no idea what was going on. Only when she spotted the bathroom window rattling in its frame did she realize that it was an earthquake.

A big one?

Maybe not?

Naked and defenseless, she wasn't able to judge the magnitude of the tremor. She wasn't used to earthquakes to begin with, seeing how rare they were in her hometown. She tried to rise to her feet, only to find herself unable. She was instead forced to clutch tightly at the side of the bathtub and look on in dismay as the water sloshed over the edge.

It must have lasted a full thirty seconds.

It felt like such an awfully long time, probably because the water continued to surge even after the shaking subsided.

In any event, she couldn't just sit around naked and vulnerable. Mustering her energy, she stood up and staggered out of the bathtub, back to the changing room.

She wiped herself dry in a daze, and by the time she came back to her senses, she had already put her clothes back on.

There were voices outside.

"Are you okay?"

"Is anyone hurt?"

She hurried out of the changing room. The hallway was still dark, but the lights in the dining room were on. As she stepped through the door, she felt as if that blinding glow was swallowing her whole.

The others were already gathered there.

"Ah, Eiko. Thank goodness you're safe," Haruka exclaimed, huddling up to her. "Are you okay?"

"A bit startled . . . "

"That was a big one, I'll say."

"I was in the bath. I didn't know what was happening at first."

"Oh . . . Your hair is still wet, you know?"

With those words, Haruka took the towel draped around her own neck and placed it on Eiko's head.

Thanks to that warm gesture, Eiko could finally glance at the various faces gathered in the dining room.

Sawa, Mizuho, Nanami—as she laid eyes on each of them, a sense of relief she had never felt before flooded through her chest.

"Is everyone here?" a voice asked.

"I think so," another answered.

Eiko stared at the girls one by one, counting to make sure that no one was missing.

"What a relief . . . "

"Everyone seems to be alright."

"Big earthquake, huh?"

"Yep. It was big, alright."

Almost everyone had already gone to bed, so they were all wearing pajamas and sweatshirts. With their tussled hair and lack of makeup, it was hard to recognize them all.

Some of them were holding hands—a sight Eiko had never seen before.

They were all in the same boat, hands joined not as part of a scene or for appearances' sake, but to act as a source of comfort for one another.

"Has it finished?"

"I don't know, but there might be aftershocks . . . "

"They're saying it's a five," one girl said, reading from her cellphone. "The epicenter was right under Tokyo . . . "

"I knew it. Tokyo gets loads of earthquakes."

"I've never felt one as strong as that before."

"Aren't the dormitory alarms supposed to go off at times like this?"

"I thought that was only if there's a fire?"

The eleven of them sat in their chairs around the dining table as they talked, each taking pauses to catch her breath and send text messages or make a quick phone call to family.

Eiko sent a message to her mother, but received no reply. No doubt she was sound asleep.

"Are earthquakes like that normal in Tokyo?" she wondered aloud.

One of the girls rose to her feet to stare out the dining room window. "It's quiet outside. Like nothing happened."

"It has to be, then. If no one's making a fuss, it can't be all that unusual."

"It's too much for me."

"I can't do this."

"Me neither. I mean, the Batman figure on my shelf got knocked to the floor."

"Oh, Saki? You like Batman?"

"He's my idol."

"Seriously? Me too!"

Eiko had never seen her costars talking so spiritedly.

She recalled the advice from the operator at the Tokyo No. 3 Consultation Room: *Why not talk things over with everyone?*

That was what she had said. She had even suggested doing it while everyone was gathered in the dining room.

"Hey, um," Eiko began, shoring up her resolve.

But at that moment—

"Ah!" someone exclaimed as the table, the chairs, even the windows, began to shake violently.

"Again?"

"An aftershock?"

Surprisingly, none of the eleven girls screamed. They didn't show even a hint of panic. There were a few audible gasps, but no one rose to their feet. They simply took the hands of the girls sitting next to them as if following a script, joining together in one large circle.

"Hold on." Maeda looked up at the warehouse ceiling. "It's not the Whiskey and Coke making my head spin. That's an earthquake," he said calmly.

"Eh? Really?" Mitsuki, on the other hand, was quite intoxicated.

Like an animal whose wild instincts had been awakened, Maeda ducked low to the ground.

"A pretty big one, too," he murmured under his breath.

The warehouse was a two-story building with a partial atrium encompassing both floors to store the larger set pieces. Naturally, they would pose a considerable threat if they collapsed, but even if those haphazardly stacked, oversized items were fine, the building was filled with so many small fragile trinkets that an earthquake of any magnitude was cause for alarm.

But there was nothing they could do to stop it.

Maeda, who had long been worried about one particular corner of the warehouse, had no other choice but to pray.

Once the first props started to fall, it didn't take long for the rest to follow.

Like dominos tipping over, several shelves collapsed in a chain reaction, triggering the rest to come crashing down in a deafening, out-of-control avalanche.

Sobering up, Mitsuki hurriedly set her glass of Whiskey and Coke on the counter and turned her back to the onrushing dust cloud, shielding her eyes and nose. Letting out a violent cough, she turned to Maeda, whose whole face—from his hair to his fine eyelashes—had been covered in white powdery dust.

For the time being, at least, the tremors seemed to have subsided.

Maeda, coughing, pulled himself to his feet and fumbled for the light switch—only to find that it had been buried behind a mound of fallen junk.

He moved instead to grab a spotlight set aside for an upcoming shoot, pointing it in the direction the avalanche had poured down from. The light streaked through the dust, falling like powdered snow.

"Look at all that dust," Mitsuki said in a muffled voice as she covered her nose and mouth.

"It isn't dust," Maeda answered, indicating further into the mass of fallen items. "See? The safety mats the stuntmen use have burst. They're feathers."

Tiny feathers fluttered through the warehouse, falling softly like in a slow-motion video. But it was something beyond the cloud of plumage, at last revealed by the spotlight, that caught her eye.

She recognized it at once.

It kind of looks like this, the director had said while scribbling a crude sketch.

Two Moons

I t was precisely 1:00 A.M.

A full day had passed since the earthquake. Having hit on her unexpected harvest, Mitsuki knocked on the door to the director's office.

"Sorry for calling you in so late," he apologized when he saw her face, though it was clear from his haggard look that he was being kept much busier than she was. "I heard you found the peanut crusher?"

"Yes," Mitsuki answered, pulling a bubble-wrapped item from her tote bag. "Some of the shelves in the warehouse collapsed during the earthquake. We found this with one of them."

The director hurried to unwrap the package. "Ah!" he exclaimed with excitement as he retrieved the contents. "Yep, this is it!"

When Mitsuki had brought him the needle-nose pliers the other day, the director had responded with an emphatic: "No, no, this is completely wrong!" As it happened, however, the peanut crusher he was looking for was itself no more than a set of pliers.

The only difference was that the tips weren't quite so thin. Instead, they were broad and flat—the perfect size for gripping a peanut in its shell. Was this really all there was to the director's much-vaunted peanut sheller?

"I got it as a souvenir on a trip," he explained.

"A trip?"

"Back in my student days."

"Um . . . " Mitsuki hesitated, a slight glower falling over her features. "Was it really in that movie you mentioned?"

"It is, yes."

"Well . . . I watched it again today, just to be sure, but I didn't see it . . . "

"Oh, it's only in the frame for a second, maybe two at most. But still, that was enough for me."

"Er . . . Do you mind if I ask why?"

"Well, it was a memento. How should I put it? It's like the . . . like the *soul* of the first movie I made back in university."

"Oh?" Mitsuki broke into a surprised frown—which was enough for the director to launch into a breathless explanation, as if someone had hit the fast-forward button.

"It was thanks to that movie that I got my foot in the door of the film industry. You see, I happened to have a friend in the US, and he invited me to visit. His hometown was in Georgia. It's this huge hodgepodge of a place, a long way south of New York . . . "

The director kept on talking.

"I didn't go there specifically to make a movie, you know? I just wanted to see the sights and record what happened on my trip. I was literally just a tourist with a video camera. I'm the one filming, though, so I'm never in the frame myself. The most I come into it is when you hear me talking a few times. Basically, my friend from Georgia takes center stage, and he wasn't bad film material, I'll tell you that. So when I started shooting, it just naturally evolved into a kind of documentary."

"Oh?" Mitsuki could barely manage a weak nod.

"Sure, I did a good job framing the shots and all that, but it all came down to the local people there. Peanut farmers, you see? I was there during harvest season, so I ended up helping out, riding at night with them in a truck loaded with peanuts, all the way to the factory. The whole while, I kept the camera rolling."

The director paused suddenly, closing his eyes.

"Then there was this big *bang*. No, more like a huge *boom*, like the car was about to explode. It wasn't that big of a truck, but it still made a decent noise. Especially when pebbles and gravel hit the chassis. But this was something different. It sounded like we were being shot at. I panicked. I mean, I had no idea what was going on. But my friend told me to relax, that we had just run over a dog. It was feral, more like a wolf. It couldn't have belonged to anyone."

The director opened his eyes.

"I had the camera running when he said that, so I caught it all perfectly—the sound, the impact, all of it. That scene ended up being the climax of the whole film. I wasn't the one driving, but I felt sorry for the dog all the same. But thanks to what happened, here I am, working in the film industry . . . "

"Yes," Mitsuki nodded as she listened to the story.

"So that's why the title is *A Dog of the South*. I added a dedication to the dog in the credits. Still, it weighs on the mind, you know?"

The director stroked the peanut crusher like a beloved pet.

"I decided that if I ever went pro and made a real movie, I'd put some kind of marker in it so I wouldn't forget about the dog. I thought I'd use this tool the peanut farmers gave me—the peanut crusher. I'd have it play a role. But I was still just an assistant director, so I talked to one of the prop guys—I think it must have been Yama back then—and asked her to put it in the background somewhere the director wouldn't notice. Somehow, it made it into the final cut. That was enough for me at the time—but I still wanted to try again when I got a chance to work on a big, expensive movie by myself. You know, up front and center, not just a quick glimpse? This was my chance, I thought. But even searching high and low, I just couldn't find it. Maybe Yama packed it away in the warehouse, I wondered, so I had a quick look around before the cameras started rolling, but no luck."

"That was when you asked me to look for it?" Mitsuki asked.

"Yeah. To be perfectly honest with you, it would have been completely pointless without the real article. But the filming schedule is basically a race against time, so I couldn't get hung up on my own sentimentality. I suppose I could always have used a lookalike. Still, I'm really glad it turned up."

Having said all this, the director paused to take a long, deep breath. Mitsuki also breathed a quiet sigh.

"In my own way, I like to think I'm remembering that dog that got run over." The director lowered his voice before continuing. "Those farmers, they told me it was for shelling peanuts, but to be perfectly frank, I don't know how you're actually supposed to do it. It just looks like an average pair of pliers to me."

"Right . . . "

"Maybe they pulled the wool over my eyes. I mean, whenever I was with them, they used their bare hands to crack the shells off. But that's just how it is. It's a memento, something to help me remember—and if they were messing with me, so be it. The dog's soul resides in this thing now. So for its sake, I want to make sure the peanut crusher appears in the movie, no matter what. Like a memorial."

Huh? Mitsuki fell to thinking. *I've seen this before.*

Was this déjà vu? She had heard those words before—*memorial, soul*—and had been left deeply touched.

When was it, exactly?

She continued to ponder that question as she left the director's office and made her way down the corridor outside the studio. *When was it? Who said it?* It wasn't long before she arrived back at the prop warehouse.

Right. I need to thank Maeda, she thought, her mind turning to a separate matter.

"I didn't do anything," Maeda explained with a warm look. "I should be the one thanking you. You seemed to enjoy that

Whiskey and Coke so much that it reminded me of the good old days."

"You like looking back over the past?" Mitsuki asked.

"Hmm." Maeda paused for a moment to ponder. "I suppose I do," he answered with a nod.

"Does that mean you're not enjoying your current job?"

"No, it's not like that. The warehouse is comfortable enough. *Szoo.* You've got everything here. Makes you feel like you're standing guard over the whole world's treasures, you know?" He trailed off, pulling a thin smile. "It's just—how should I put this?—I like *people*. Mixing drinks in some little corner of Tokyo, you get to meet all sorts of folks. *Szoo.* Night after night, you get to talk to them. All strangers, mind you. It was fun, really . . . Yep, those were the good old days."

Mitsuki's next words poured out before she had a chance to think. "In that case, why don't you do it again?"

"What?"

"Bartending."

"Huh?" He glanced across at her as though looking at some inscrutable sight. "I'm retired."

"Ah. I see . . . "

"So that's that."

"From what you said yesterday, it sounded like you just sort of ended up managing the warehouse without even meaning to."

"Yeah. Well. I'm getting too old for bartending now."

"Do you think so? Young, handsome bartenders are nice and all, but it's kind of romantic when an experienced silver fox makes you a drink, you know?"

"Really?"

"If I knew a place with a bartender like that, I'd go there every day," Mitsuki answered playfully.

To tell the truth, she couldn't hold even the smallest of drinks, so she wouldn't really drop by all that often. Yesterday's

Whiskey and Coke, however, was like something from another dimension, much more than the sum of its parts. How could such a miraculous beverage be concocted simply by mixing together ordinary ingredients?

"You're a professional. That's all there is to it," Mitsuki declared.

Maeda raised his chin, his eyes closing in gratitude. "You think so?"

"I do."

"Hmm . . ."

Having unearthed the peanut crusher, Mitsuki was able to take the next day off free of worry. She decided to stop by Ibaragi, the antiques shop in Shimokitazawa that she had visited the other night. The needle-nose pliers might not have been what the director was looking for, but she wanted to thank the owner all the same.

If she was being honest with herself, however, she would have recognized that she was just making excuses, and that what she really wanted was to visit that strange shop without work hanging over her head.

The business card the owner had given her said that the store opened at 9:00 P.M. Buoyed by her good mood, she ended up arriving at eight forty, but to her surprise, the lights were on inside. It was already open.

She found Ibaragi sitting quietly in the back of the store, just as he had been the other day. He looked sleepy, and was constantly rubbing his eyes as if to keep himself awake.

"Excuse me," Mitsuki called out.

"Ah. The woman from the other day," he sleepily acknowledged her.

Perhaps she should be thankful he remembered her? Mitsuki waited for her eyes to adjust to the dimly-lit store, then gave Ibaragi a second look over. His right hand rested on the desk in front of him, a white bandage wrapped around the base of his thumb.

"Apologies," he said, bowing his head for some reason.

"Not at all," sounded the only response to come to mind.

There shouldn't have been anything for him to apologize to her for, but now that he had uttered the words, she felt obliged to ask why. "What happened?"

"It's tendinitis," Ibaragi answered regretfully. "This arrived recently," he said, pointing to a small telescope on his desk. "I called it a *moonlight amplifier*, but when I set about polishing it, I couldn't stop myself."

"I see . . ."

"Sorry, but I've forgotten your name. I know you gave me a business card . . . You're from a film studio, the prop department, right?"

"Yes. Mitsuki Sawatari."

"Mitsuki. That's a nice name. Do you mind if I call you that?"

What? She was taken aback slightly at the abruptness of his question, but having been complimented so nicely, she couldn't ask that he stand on ceremony.

"Um, if you're sure." No sooner did those nonsensical words leave her mouth than her face turned hot, and she averted her gaze.

"Do you know how to apply medicine or a bandage to your dominant hand, Mitsuki? Or maybe I should ask if you live alone first?"

"I do . . ."

"Right. As you can see, I've used a compress instead of a bandage. I'm by myself here, and I'm a trueborn right-hander, you see."

"Yes." Mitsuki almost broke out into a laugh at his peculiar way of speaking. What on earth did he mean by a *trueborn right-hander*?

"I'm not sure if I should say this, but I'm pretty sure my right hand is more dexterous than most people's. My left hand is just as clumsy as anyone else's, though. Really, it's border-line useless. So I can't begin to explain how difficult it was dressing the wound and applying the compress, all with my left hand."

"Yes." She couldn't hold back the smile pulling at the edges of her mouth.

What's with this guy? He is *pretty funny, but he's a bit of an odd sort.*

"It took forever. About thirty minutes, I'd say. It was gruel-ing, let me tell you. My right hand is the tool of my trade, and it's also my kryptonite. Using just my left hand, it's like life is moving in slow-motion."

"Ah yes. I suppose it would be." Mitsuki didn't really know how to respond to this confession, and so found herself going along with him.

"Anyway, I figured everything was going to take me longer than usual today, so I came into the store thirty minutes early. I thought it would take longer to set up, but I managed to raise the shutters with my left hand and ended up opening ahead of time. But that all meant getting up earlier today . . . And, well, you see, I have a condition. It makes me sleepy during the day and keeps me active at night. *Bat syndrome*, I call it. But I didn't get enough sleep, and now all I want to do is get some more shuteye."

"Yes, I can see. You look exhausted."

"That bad, is it?" Ibaragi rubbed the back of his head with his good hand. "Well, the work might have been slow moving, but the job's done. I managed to polish the moonlight amplifier and finetune it. It's ready to be put up for sale."

"What does it do?" Mitsuki asked, impelled by a stroke of luck.

"What does it do?" Ibaragi repeated, picking up the

moonlight amplifier while cradling his injured hand. "Take a look, please."

At his prompting, Mitsuki placed her right eye on the eyepiece, but it was too dark and blurry to make anything out.

"You can't see anything, can you?" Ibaragi surmised. "It's like that indoors. It's meant for observing the moon, after all. Yes, it's only when you point it at the night sky that it really comes into its own. I checked the sky before opening up shop, but I couldn't find the moon. It must be a cloudy night."

Around here? Mitsuki was tempted to ask aloud, but Ibaragi was so earnest in his explanation that she followed on in wordless silence.

"But so long as the moon is out, it's a real marvel. If you look up into the sky with it, you can see *two* moons. Of course, there's only one when you look at it with the naked eye. But when you observe it through this device, there are always two of them. Pretty cool, huh?"

Eh? In her surprise, Mitsuki almost spoke her thoughts out aloud. *Doesn't that just mean it's out of focus? You can end up with double vision if the focus is off, but that's all there is to it . . .*

"Do you know the significance of being able to see two moons, Mitsuki? It means that this planet we're on, this city, maybe even we ourselves—there might be two of everything."

I don't think that's what it means . . . But maybe he'll think I'm a grouch if I say anything. Does he actually believe that? Or is he just trying to put a positive spin on a piece of junk? I don't know . . . But it is *interesting.*

"What if there's another Tokyo, another world, another *me*—one who doesn't have tendinitis, or even my bat syndrome? Instead of living only at night, maybe that other me is out smiling in the light of day? This isn't just because of the moonlight amplifier, but sometimes I wonder if that isn't the truth of the world."

Having heard Ibaragi out to the end, Mitsuki felt something

pop inside her chest. *Huh? Didn't someone else say something like that?*

She had felt just like this after the director's talk of memory and souls.

Ah, now I get it.

Her thoughts slipped into place, and at the same time, she realized that when Ibaragi had asked if she lived alone, it was because he had caught a glimpse of her fingers, not because he was telling her about his hand.

Finally grasping all this, she quietly hid the ring still firmly attached to her left ring finger.

On the western outskirts of Tokyo was a small town, on the western-most fringes of which could be found a small movie theater called the Third Cinema House.

Shuro stood on the sidewalk in front of the building, chuckling to himself as he stared up at the moonless night sky.

I can't believe I came all this way. I must be out of my mind.

He glanced down at his watch. It was nearly nine o'clock.

There was still time before the screening got underway. He had already purchased his ticket, and there was nothing else that needed his attention. As such, he found himself standing beneath a lamppost in a strange corner of the city, flicking through the pamphlet he had received with his ticket.

The Disappearing Man. That was the title of the film he was about to see. Shuro didn't know the name of the director or the lead actress. He knew only that it had been made roughly half a century ago, and that the pamphlet said of it: *Not even the most discerning moviegoers will have heard of this hidden gem.*

There was no record of the film ever having been screened, yet an old reel of it had turned up in this movie theater's storage warehouse. According to the pamphlet, this might very well be the first time it was being shown anywhere in the country, at least as far as the cinema could tell. It had apparently been put into storage sometime after its completion, and the theater staff were still investigating why it had gone unnoticed for so long.

Shuro's interest, however, had little to do with such cinephilic concerns. Rather, his father played the role of a veterinary clinic director, the second-most important character in the film. He had happened on this information by chance while searching his father's name on the internet, where the title had come up as *Now showing*. Of course, he wouldn't be able to tell whether it really was his father until he watched it for himself. That being said, to the best of his knowledge, there were no other actors who shared his father's name, so it was probably safe to assume that it was actually him.

The pamphlet was about the size of a small paperback, a trifling eight pages in length. Yet the more Shuro read, the more absorbed he found himself in the cinema's commentary. Before he knew it, he was greedily devouring each and every word in the light of the streetlamp.

The setting is a downtown area alongside a river, and the story begins when a man is brought into a small veterinary clinic at the end of an alleyway. The man, washed downstream, is found on the river's bank, barely breathing. Mitsuyo, a nurse working at the veterinary clinic, finds him and brings him in with the help of several men working at a nearby factory. The clinic director is a skilled veterinarian, but he's also a heavy drinker, always reeking of alcohol . . .

Having read that far, Shuro peeled his gaze away. The description was so detailed it might spoil the movie, so he decided to read the rest later. Just before he could put the document away, however, a column titled *About the Cast* caught his eye. The column didn't just describe the lead actress, but also Shuro's father—or at the very least, the actor he assumed was his father.

Ryuichiro Tashiro, who has played parts as varied as chivalrous yakuza bosses and down-on-their-luck aristocrats, shines here in his supporting role as the clinic director.

Really? Shuro couldn't believe his eyes. A quick scan of the biographical data and previous roles all but guaranteed that this was indeed his father.

But Shuro had never heard of any films in which his father played a *chivalrous yakuza boss* or a *down-on-his-luck aristocrat*. In fact, he wasn't familiar with *any* movies featuring that sort of character.

There was still time before the screening, so Shuro presented his ticket to enter the theater and looked around the shabby lobby. It wasn't long before he found a middle-aged man in a black suit whom he took to be the manager. "Excuse me," he said. "Could you tell me who wrote this?"

"Ah." The man pointed to an absentminded-looking youth in a corner of the lobby. "That would be him."

"Hey," Shuro called out.

"Yes?" The youth looked up. When his eyes met Shuro's, a nostalgic look fell across his face, as if he was witnessing a fond memory playing back in the most unexpected of ways.

The hour was rapidly approaching 1:00 A.M.

Shuro had been so caught up in the conversation that he had let time slip away from him. But he wasn't just interested in the movie—the youth himself had caught his attention.

When the screening ended a little after eleven o'clock, Shuro had made his way to the lobby, where the young man was still working.

"Um," he spoke up, impressed—or rather, intrigued—by the pamphlet's contents.

The youth seemed to be even more familiar with Shuro's father, Ryuichiro Tashiro, than Shuro himself was. Shuro had no idea what these *chivalrous yakuza boss* and *down-on-his-luck aristocrat* roles were, but if there was any chance that he might be able to see those movies . . . He had so many questions.

Shuro had never expected that another person could know his father's career better than he himself did, nor that he would have an opportunity to speak with them directly. He had certainly never found himself in this situation before.

Yet the youth politely brushed his questions aside. "I'm sorry, but I'm working right now. If you can wait another half hour, I'll be happy to discuss it with you," he answered in a low voice.

"Also, I should apologize in advance," he added. "Ryuichiro Tashiro played a yakuza boss in a film called *Unto Paradise*, and the fallen aristocrat was from another called *Tomorrow's Sunset*. I might have given the impression that I had actually seen them, but I'm afraid I haven't. Unfortunately, I haven't been able to find copies of either one."

To Shuro's surprise, the youth casually dropped the titles of two other films in which his father had appeared.

He decided to wait in the lobby until the youth's shift was over, after which the young man led him to his favorite late-night bar.

As they made their way through the town, the youth started telling him about the bar, a place called The Revolving Lantern, demonstrating once more his natural aptitude for storytelling.

"It's really dark in there," he began. "Not the owner. There's nothing wrong with his personality or anything. No, I mean it's literally *dark* in there. It takes you a while just to be able to see your own hands. I work in a movie theater, but even I get caught out by how dimly lit the place is."

When they opened the doors and stepped inside, that description was borne out in reality. Shuro had had cause to visit a good many rough venues during his career, so he was immune to the kind of darkness that might leave a regular person virtually paralyzed—but even he hesitated for a moment before entering. He couldn't even find his footing.

He stood there, waiting for his eyes to adjust, when the youth, already familiar with the bar, stepped forward. "This way," he said, pushing deeper into the building. Shuro followed behind him, relying on the citrusy scent of his cologne to find his way through the dark.

But even after walking five or six meters, Shuro could sense no sign of people drinking, of alcohol, glasses, or anything else one might expect to find in a bar.

"What on earth is this place?" he mumbled.

Perhaps his eyes had finally adjusted to the darkness, as he finally managed to make out a set of barstools and what must have been the bartender illuminated in the soft glow of a faint bluish-white light.

"Welcome!" the silhouetted figure said in polite greeting.

"Evening," the youth responded in kind.

The bluish-white light slowly revealed a long counter complete with a row of tall, slender chairs. As they took their seats, Shuro remarked to himself that while gloomy inside, the place did indeed resemble a simple bar. That being said, the distance between the entrance and the counter was certainly strange, and the fact that there wasn't even a single light source to guide patrons down the passageway in between was stranger still.

"All that stuff I wrote in the pamphlet—I was basically winging it. So . . . I can call you Tashiro, right?"

"Yes," Shuro answered, peering into the youth's face, blurry and indistinct in the poor light.

"What I'm trying to say, Tashiro, is I'm not really all that familiar with what kind of actor your father was."

Their drinks soon arrived on the counter, and without offering up a toast, they each took a sip. *Not bad,* Shuro almost found himself whispering out loud.

"Then how did you know all that?" he asked.

"I'm always going to the library," the youth answered, turning back to his story. "The local library round these parts has all these old film magazines, so I copied most of what I wrote in the pamphlet from them."

"I see . . . " Shuro nodded, savoring the sweet scent of his drink. He was impressed—the youth was already halfway to becoming a detective himself.

The local library round these parts—judging from his choice of phrase, the youth probably wasn't a local. Perhaps he had only moved here recently. From his interactions with the bartender, he didn't come across as a regular customer.

Judging that it would be safe to push a little further, Shuro was about to ask the youth a follow-up question, when he realized that he didn't even know his name.

"Er, I don't think I heard your name," he ventured.

"Ah, sorry," the youth answered, resting his glass on the counter. "It's Fuyuki. Ren Fuyuki," he said, straightening his posture as someone might when offering a business card.

"Ren," Shuro repeated. "Well then, if you don't mind my asking, are you new in town?"

"Yes," Ren replied. Then, taking another sip from his glass as if to gather his resolve, he added: "It's a little complicated . . . There's something I need to take care of. Nothing too serious, mind you." He paused there, lowering his voice. "I've been traveling about since I left home, getting by on odd jobs."

"Since you left home?" Shuro repeated.

"Well, I guess I ran away." The youth's voice dropped even further. "I was keeping an eye on the bulletin board in the middle of town, and I saw an opening at the theater for a part-time job."

"You like cinema?"

"Cinema? More like movie theaters themselves. They're one of very few safe refuges in a huge city like this. I've always been drawn to dark places. Huh. I guess that includes this bar, too."

"Is your main job to write leaflets and the like, then?"

"As if," Ren snorted, staring back at him in surprise. "I'm a part-timer. Basically, that means I'm responsible for anything and everything."

Though Shuro was publicly hailed as a great detective, in actual fact, he remained quite ignorant of what most people in society regarded as common knowledge. He had no idea, for instance, how to use a coin laundry, how savings accounts worked, or what *fortified milk* actually meant.

"I do practically everything at the theater, from selling tickets to cooking hot dogs at the snack bar." The youth's voice returned to its previous volume. "The manager you saw earlier—he's not a bad guy, but he hardly does any actual work. He doesn't know much about movies, either."

"Huh? Really?" Shuro startled.

"What kind of work do you do, Tashiro?" the youth asked all of a sudden.

At times like this, Shuro's habit was to pick from one of his many former part-time jobs, like a clerk at a pachinko parlor, a cook at a boxed lunch supplier, or a barista at a station-side café. And yet, he came out with an answer that he would never have expected to share with a virtual stranger: "Actually, I'm training to be an actor."

"Ah. I knew it," the youth answered, accepting the lie hook, line, and sinker. "I know how you feel. I always wanted to take over my father's business."

"Oh? What does your father do?"

"Both my parents died while I was just a kid, though. I was in my first year of middle school at the time. They were on their way back from a relative's funeral. My dad was driving. On the expressway. At night. Apparently, a truck hit the car at high speed, sending it flying and bursting into flames . . . I didn't hear the gory details. But anyway, our aunt and uncle took care of us after that."

"Us?"

"Yeah. Me and my sister."

"You have a sister?"

"Yeah. I guess she must be doing fine. Probably. She's two years older than me. Huh. Thirty-eight this year."

"Eh?" Shuro's body jerked upright in surprise. "Hold on a second, Ren. You're thirty-six?"

"Sure am. If I'm still living, that is."

"If you're still living?"

Shuro panicked, his mind racing with theories as to whether this eerily dark bar and its ill-omened name—The Revolving Lantern—had anything to do with that comment about being still alive.

"I'm just kidding," Ren answered, waving a hand in front of his face in apology. "Ah, but you're right about my age. Yes,

I'm thirty-six. I've hardly grown-up at all over the last ten years, though."

On closer inspection, Shuro could see that what he had initially taken to be a youthful countenance had indeed receded slightly. Was this what people called the sunset years of youth?

Shuro, however, was in exactly the same boat—he too looked like he hadn't aged a day since he was twenty-four. Most people he met assumed that, at the very least, he couldn't be older than thirty.

Shuro himself was morbidly averse to the idea of growing old. He didn't mind at all if people looked down on him as a greenhorn—and in fact, he quite liked it when they did. It made some aspects of his work that much easier.

"Every now and then, I think about surprising my sister. Like, I wonder how she might react if I just turned up at our old apartment tomorrow, looking the same way I did twelve years ago."

"Are you planning to go home, one day?" Shuro asked in a more polite tone, almost laughing at himself when he realized that Ren wasn't quite as young as his appearance might suggest.

"No, I don't think so. It's just a dream. A fantasy."

"But why not?"

"That one's easy. I'd just end up being too dependent on my sister. Because that's the kind of person she is. She's always there to lend you an ear, and she can solve pretty much any problem that comes her way. I stopped growing, you know? Like I was stagnant . . . No, I shouldn't blame her for everything. Anyway, I wanted to distance myself from her, for my own sake. So I could be a better person." Ren broke into a frown as he took his next sip. "But as you can see, in the end, I haven't grown at all."

Behind the counter, the shadowy bartender stood in silence, polishing one glass after the next. The squeak of the dry cloth rubbing against the glass echoed around the two men like a background chorus.

Shuro remained on guard, expecting Ren to ask him about

himself next, and so turned away, pretending to be distracted by the bartender. All the same, if the other man had ventured to ask him directly, he might have volunteered a truthful answer: *I'm looking for movies my father appeared in.*

As a child, he had never been particularly interested in his father's career—but at some point, he had started trying to re-assemble all those stray pieces left behind. In any event, Shuro wasn't fit to judge whether someone had grown stagnant in their personal development.

Though they might find fame for effortlessly solving com-plicated problems when it came to other people, detectives like him were often hopeless at solving the mysteries surrounding their own lives.

"I'm sorry I couldn't be of much help," Ren said.

"Not at all." Shuro shook his head. "You helped me realize that I never bothered to research old movie magazines."

"Well, for my part," Ren began, emptying his glass, "like I wrote in the pamphlet, I want to keep on researching why ex-actly the theater was holding onto a copy of that film."

This man might have what it takes to be a better detective than he himself did, Shuro thought with a grin.

"Thanks," he said, not sure whether he was addressing Ren or the shadowy bartender. In any case, he left a bill to cover the drinks on the counter.

"Shall I call you a taxi?" Ren asked.

Without really understanding why, Shuro shook his head, quickly pulling away.

The darkness seemed somewhat gentler than when he had first entered the building, but still he made sure to continue in a straight line down the pitch-black corridor, hand outstretched, until he finally brushed up against what felt like a wooden door.

The door, however, was firmly stuck.

He tried jerking it open with all his might, as if to break free from the darkness looming around him.

Yet the effect was quite the opposite. A mass of darkness took on human form. Shuro stumbled to his feet as he lost his center of gravity, seemingly snatched up by some monstrous entity.

This, however, could perhaps be attributed to his having drunk a little too much.

Whatever the cause, he somehow managed to make it outside—only to immediately regret not having taken Ren up on his offer to call a taxi.

He rummaged through his pocket for a handkerchief to wipe the sweat from his forehead, but his fingers touched instead the cold surface of a business card. "What the . . . ?" he murmured as he pulled it out.

Night Taxi: Blackbird.

"Right, him . . . "

He had felt like walking home the last time, and so hadn't followed up with the taxi driver. Since then, he had felt somewhat guilty each time his thoughts took him back to that night. He wanted to apologize, if he ever had the chance. Still, there was no guarantee that the driver would be willing to come all this way to the outskirts of Tokyo . . . Ah, but it was worth a shot, he decided. He punched the number from the business card into his cellphone, but the moment it started to ring, a yellow taxi with a glowing red vacant sign began to approach from further down the street.

Divine intervention?

Reflexively, he hung up the call and raised a hand into the air to hail the cab.

Well, tonight was a letdown, Matsui thought as he parked the car at one of his favorite break spots. There was a local bus terminal nearby, along with a park equipped with a restroom where he could freshen up.

There were always a few nights every year—this one included—when he failed to find so much as a single customer.

Tokyo could be a curious place. Sometimes, he would pick up the same passengers again and again, wondering if this really was a sprawling metropolis, and sometimes, he would find himself asking where everyone had gone. It could be almost terrifying, the thought that everyone had just vanished without a trace, leaving him entirely alone like the main character in a sci-fi film he saw once as a child.

Matsui cut the engine, reclined his seat, and stretched his body, staring into the night sky outside.

There wasn't a star to be seen.

Of course, like the people of this city, there had to be countless stars out there, but for whatever reason, tonight, they all seemed to have vanished.

You can't afford to be too greedy on days like this, he reminded himself, when he glanced at his cellphone.

At that moment, it started to ring—an unknown number.

"You've got to be kidding me," he muttered.

The call, however, ended after just one ring.

But who . . . ?

In nine cases out of ten, when someone called him directly, they were one of his regular clients—but as he had their numbers registered in his address book, their full name should have been displayed on the screen. Yet it wasn't. Either someone had dialed the wrong number, or this was a new customer he had given a business card to.

Matsui found himself recalling the face of Kanako Fuyuki, and stopped himself. She was his most recently registered regular client, so if it had been her, her name would have been front and center.

But what if . . . ?

He glanced down at the clock.

It was almost two in the morning.

Still too early. Or rather, not early at all.

If memory served correctly, her workday ended at 7:00 A.M..

Or was it more accurate to say that her day *began* at seven? There was little point making empty plans, but he *would* like to invite her to the diner again, to take a short reprieve from reality and enjoy a hearty breakfast together. After all, it was that kind of night. He didn't have any other customers to pick up.

He opened his list of contacts and—

"No," he thought, shaking his head and locking his screen.

She would still be working in the call center at this time of night. There was little chance that she would stop to take a call on her private cellphone.

Hold on a second. He unlocked his screen once more and brought up her contact entry. Next to her private number was another belonging to the Tokyo No. 3 Consultation Room.

"If you ever need to talk, feel free to call this number any time."

Yes, she had said that just after giving him her business card.

The number, of course, was the main line at the Tokyo No. 3 Consultation Room, famous throughout the city as a sanctuary for lost souls. Fuyuki was probably still working, so he decided to give the number a call. If he was lucky enough to be put through to her, he could change his voice a little so she wouldn't recognize him as Matsui from Blackbird.

Yes, this could be fun.

After all, he too was a denizen of Tokyo.

"We get a lot of calls from taxi drivers," he remembered her saying. "It sounds like a stressful line of work."

And if . . .

If they could go and have breakfast together again, Matsui would take pleasure in that fresh meeting in and of itself. At the same time, he could anticipate the conversation turning back to the topic of her missing brother. From there, he would be able to reveal a secret that he had never shared with anyone, that he too was looking for someone.

Yes, this was perfect. After all, it was her job to listen to unshareable truths, and no doubt she would give him some kind of answer or solution.

"Actually, I'm . . . " he began, running through the scenario in his mind. "Actually, I'm a taxi driver, you see. I had a customer once whose face I've never been able to forget—a woman. I know it's stupid of me to feel this way, but I'd love to be able to meet her again. Yes, I know full well that I should keep these feelings to myself, that I risk breaking the trust my customers place in me. But I just don't know how to move past her."

No, there was no way she would be able to give a clear answer to such an absurd problem. She would probably end up responding with mute bewilderment.

Give it up.

But what if—

Give it up, already.

But there might *be a chance . . .*

Shuro gave his home address to the driver of the yellow taxi.

"Ah, yes. Past the police box on the corner there, then up to the pizza place. Keep going past the convenience store and liquor shop and turn right, yes? A friend of mine used to live right around there."

The driver, it seemed, was a little *too* familiar with the area.

According to his nameplate, his name was Daisuke Nagasawa. Judging from the fast-paced lilt of his voice, he was a natural-born Edoite. Of course, this was entirely Shuro's own deduction, but he was practically certain.

Estimated age: forty-eight years old. He must have married late, as he had a five-year-old daughter, a sweet little thing and her father's pride and joy. How did Shuro know all this? From a small piece of paper, around the size of a business card, taped to a corner of the dashboard, emblazoned with freshly learned, clumsy handwriting reading *You can do it, Daddy*.

Nagasawa's hobby was memorizing road maps from all over

Japan. Starting with the twenty-three wards of Tokyo, he had an intricate, near-perfect understanding of the various nearby cities and prefectures. On top of that, he liked to add to his knowledge miscellaneous pieces of trivia gleamed from his passengers, from the radio, from sports newspapers and the like, to point out hidden stories of one place or another as the car made its way through an ocean of mundane scenery.

It was all so excessive and over the top. This Nagasawa seemed to know everything, from the best classic ramen restaurants to the precise addresses of twenty-four-hour supermarkets and even the gated private residences of big-name politicians.

"Do you happen to know a yakisoba noodle store called Daimon?" Shuro asked, mentioning a restaurant he used to frequent.

"Of course," the driver answered immediately.

"What about a café called Flag?"

"Yes, I know it," he said, reciting not only the street address, but the phone number too.

"What about all-night diners?" Shuro asked vaguely.

"Ah, diners. The list is always changing, but I've got around six hundred different places in my head at any given time. Let me know what you want, and I'll be happy to take you there."

"Really?" Shuro tried to restrain himself, but his mouth seemed to move of its own accord. "There was a place around Iwabuchi in Akabane, called *Kitchen Aya*, I think. I haven't been there in ages, but I could kill for one of their ham-and-egg sets."

"Ah. That one's closed down," Nagasawa answered decisively. "The owner is running another diner now with three other women, a place called Yotsukado, at the intersection in Katatokicho. It's very nice."

Truth be told, Shuro already knew that Ayano's old store had closed down. He had seen it for himself while exploring the area around the apartment where he used to live.

But he was nonetheless taken aback.

He had assumed Kitchen Aya would always be there, and that Ayano herself would keep on happily preparing those ham-and-egg sets like always.

No. No doubt she was still making them, even now. He had always believed she would set up a new diner, uniquely her own.

"In Katatokicho . . . " Shuro murmured.

"Do you want to go there?" Nagasawa asked. "It *is* a really nice diner. It's open till morning, so it's quite popular with my taxi driver friends. I go there myself, sometimes."

Shuro pretended to hesitate for a moment before answering. "Maybe I'll give it a try, then."

Listening to this overly talkative driver had made him hungry, in any event.

No, he was just making excuses now, Shuro reprimanded himself. But if Ayano really was there, he would love to talk to her again.

Shuro stared through the taxi window into the dark Tokyo sky.

There wasn't a star to be found.

Blue Staircases

It was already 1:00 A.M.

What time did she go to bed and what time did she wake up? When did the day begin and at what point did it end?

When you worked day after day, night after night, for as long as Ayano had, you started to forget.

She had grown used to life working at an all-night diner, but on her days off, she just didn't know what to do with herself.

It was already dark when she woke up, and midnight by the time she finished the household chores—certainly no hour to go out and meet up with friends.

If there was someone she really wanted to see, she could force herself to take only a short nap in the morning and set her alarm for noon. But on her days off, Ayano tended to sleep much longer than usual. The next thing she knew, it would be midnight, and she only had one friend still up and about at that hour—Ichiko.

Ichiko lived in Shimokitazawa, where she worked from home, making accessories. She had a habit of staying up all through the night. Her apartment was right behind a shopping arcade, so even at this late hour, she could quickly shoot out to grab a snack whenever the fancy struck her.

Practically by reflex, Ayano got ready to leave. Yes, she wanted to go see Ichiko—but more than that, she wanted something to eat.

Or rather, her body was itching to go outside. It was that simple.

From Sasazuka, where Ayano lived, it was a brisk twenty-minute walk to Shimokitazawa. The shortest path was to head south following a more-or-less direct route, but that meant passing through dark and unnerving residential areas. As such, whenever Ayano went to meet Ichiko in the middle of the night, she would keep her cellphone pressed up against her ear, murmuring phrases like *I'm on my way* or *I'm just passing Inokashira Street*.

So she did the same this time too, pulling out her phone and dialing Ichiko.

"Yeah?" came the sleepy voice on the other end of the line.

"Are you still up?" Ayano asked.

"Ayano? Where are you?" came Ichiko's response, so clear she might have been standing right beside her.

"I'm nearly at Inokashira Street."

"It isn't raining, is it?"

"Rain?" She stared upward, but there was no rain—no stars, no clouds, no moon either. Nothing but a bland, unremarkable sky. "No rain here."

"Was today your day off?"

"Yes. I woke up in the middle of the night, and I didn't have any plans."

Still talking on the phone, she stepped out onto the sidewalk at Inokashira Street, the road busy with traffic even at this late hour.

"Ah, you just reached the main road, right?" Ichiko exclaimed cheerfully. "I can hear the cars passing by."

"I'm there now," Ayano reported as she crossed at the pedestrian lights, her pace unchanging as the cars streamed by behind her.

"Hey," Ichiko began. "I've been meaning to say something for a while, but chatting on the phone like this really isn't a good idea, you know? You might lose track of your surroundings if you get too caught up in conversation. You don't know what you could walk into."

"I'll be okay. I'm keeping my eyes open."

"So you calling me isn't really the main event here?"

"Basically."

She had to keep Ichiko talking. After all, the surrounding darkness seemed to creep in when the silences stretched out too long.

"I haven't seen you in a while," she remarked.

"Yeah. I took a little break from work," Ichiko answered with a sigh.

"You did?"

"I've just been so tired lately . . . But I guess the truth is that orders have been slowing down. If things don't turn around soon, it won't be long before I can't even pay the rent. I've gotta start thinking about what comes next, you know?"

"Oh. So you weren't working tonight?"

"Nope. I was asleep. Hey, hold on. Right. I'm back home in Shikoku."

"Eh?"

"I said I went back home. With business the way it is, I thought I'd better talk it over with my folks."

"Wait, what? Hold on a second. So you're not in Shimokitazawa?"

"That's what I said."

"Then what was all that about Inokashira Street?"

"Sorry. I was half asleep. Your call woke me up, and, well, you know me. I completely forgot where I was."

All of a sudden, the temperature had suddenly plunged a full two degrees.

Ayano hurried her pace.

She was still in the middle of a residential area, with some distance yet to go before she reached the commercial district. She had to keep on talking, but she couldn't think of anything to say. The space around her seemed to warp, closing in. Normally, she would stay on the phone all the way to Ichiko's apartment.

"Ah, I'm here," she would say. "Just outside your apartment building. I'm going up the stairs now. I can already see the door. There you are!"

Then, Ichiko would open the door to greet her. Yes, this kind of conversation worked wonders to relieve Ayano's anxiety as she slowly approached her friend's well-lit room.

Hearing that Ichiko had gone back to her hometown, it was like a light in Ayano's head had been snuffed out. She had been left behind, alone.

"Wait, please," Ayano said, composing herself. "Don't hang up just yet. Not until I get to the shopping arcade."

"Sure. No problem."

Ichiko knew better than anyone just how uncomfortable Ayano was walking around town alone in the dead of night.

"Have you seen anyone lately?" Ichiko asked.

"Yes. I bumped into Haruka the other day. What a shock! She's a real-life actress now."

"So she's already made her debut?"

"Not yet. But she's starring in an upcoming film."

This alleyway is super dark! Ayano felt like complaining. Being night-blind since birth, dark places looked to her completely black.

"A movie? Woah. Way to go Haruka."

"But apparently, there's a lot going on. It sounds pretty stressful."

"What about you, Ayano? How's everything on your end?"

"Me? With work, you mean?"

"When is it not work with you?"

"What do you mean?"

Ayano realized her thoughts were still all over the place. Ichiko was right. Ever since she had started working at her current diner, she had barely spoken to her friends about *anything* other than work. In the past, she would discuss her love life, much the same as any young woman, but recently, her conversations seemed to be limited to the diner, to whether business was going well or not. The same should have been the case now, and yet . . . Ayano herself was starting to lose track of everything.

But no, it wasn't because of work that she had felt like stepping out to see Ichiko after so long. She really didn't have anything at all to talk about on the business front.

"Hey. Are you okay?" Ichiko asked, speaking more loudly in response to Ayano's long silence.

"Yeah, I'm fine. I was just thinking."

"About what?"

"About what I must have been thinking."

"So you *did* have something else in mind?"

"Probably, yes."

At that moment, Ayano's vision was filled with images of Tashiro, who used to frequent her old diner for the ham-and-egg sets.

"Hold on a second," she said, coming to a stop and glancing about.

"What now?" Ichiko was starting to sound worried.

"Um . . . I think I'm lost."

"Eh? But it's a straight road."

"Yeah, I know. But I still haven't made it to the shopping arcade. And there's something weird here . . . A shop? It's so dark out, but the lights are on inside."

"Huh? A food place? It's probably a bar or something."

"No." Ayano approached the store and checked the sign. "Looks like it's called *Ibaragi*. Have you heard of it?"

"Nope. Where exactly are you?"

"I don't know." Ayano shook her head.

Nonetheless, the store, Ibaragi, had appeared with perfect timing, filling Ayano's heart with an eerie, indescribable feeling.

"Sorry. I'm going to have to hang up," came a woman's voice from the storefront.

Ibaragi looked up from his work desk to find a petite woman peering inside with an apprehensive look on her face.

He had never seen her before; this was a first-time customer.

"Welcome!" he said in a low, small voice.

The woman startled, turning toward the source of the voice—but just like the street outside, to her eyes, the store was impenetrably dark.

"Excuse me," she said falteringly, calling back in his general direction.

Ibaragi, in his usual manner, glanced toward the woman without really looking, thinking: *Maybe she doesn't know what kind of shop this is?*

He rubbed the base of his thumb, still sore from his tendinitis. "Um, you know . . . " he began, making the rare move of speaking up first. "We're actually a—"

"A secondhand shop, right?" She still couldn't make them out clearly, but that didn't stop Ayano from curiously examining the items lined up on the shelves.

Huh? Caught off guard, Ibaragi stood up straight to make himself more presentable.

Most female customers opted for the terms *antiques store* or *vintage shop*. Then again, Ibaragi himself could never quite decide what his store ought to be called. If he had to settle on a label, he too would probably go with *secondhand shop*.

At any rate, there was no doubt that the products he sold were all old. He liked to think that they were all capable of serving some new, active purpose out there in the world, but he was fully aware that this was largely a vain fantasy on his part. Perhaps, he sometimes asked himself, he was only forcing his own dreams onto the myriad items?

Ayano, on the other hand, braced herself, wondering whether she might not have been swallowed up by some mystifying fairy tale.

I mean, I was on my way to the shopping arcade . . .

After all, what were the chances of finding a place like this, open for business in the middle of the night in what wasn't even a commercial area? It didn't make any sense.

Yes, she was starting to think that it was all a dream.

Mentally, she retraced her steps. She had fallen to sleep exhausted, woken up without feeling refreshed, then stepped outside and called Ichiko. But she could hardly believe that Ichiko would actually go back to Shikoku. She had always maintained that she would never, *ever*, move back to her hometown.

"Um . . . " Ayano, her eyes slowly adjusting to the dim murk, stared blankly at Ibaragi. "Er . . . This isn't a dream, is it?"

"Huh?" he answered, struggling to maintain his composure. *She's a perceptive one, that's for sure . . .*

He was just thinking to himself that this store existed solely to support his dreams, and here she was asking him just that out of the blue. It wouldn't be entirely correct to answer *Yes, this is my dream*, but it wouldn't necessarily be wrong, either.

"Well, I guess you could call it a dream, in a sense," he answered.

"Ah, I knew it." Ayano sighed, taking his answer at face value.

The truth was, it scared her to think what she had found herself in, if this were actually real.

In the back of the darkened store, there appeared a man with a compress wrapped around his right hand, like a pale apparition coming into focus. How odd. Ayano likewise had a white dressing wrapped around the fingers of her right hand after cutting them at work. She had difficulty making out the various objects on the shelves, but everything seemed so old and lifeless, none of it making a shred of sense—as indeed one might expect in a dream.

Ibaragi, for his part, broke into a warm smile at this reaction. *At last,* he thought.

Long had he dreamed of an encounter like this.

Most people saw his actions and his beliefs as strange, eccentric. But one day, he had always hoped, he would meet someone who understood him—and if they turned out to be a woman, perhaps she would be the partner he had always been searching for.

This wasn't just mere *understanding*.

No, his feelings now could be summed up in only one way: *I knew it.*

The fact that those same words came to the woman so naturally suggested that their minds were already closely aligned, that she too had been scouring the world for someone with whom she could share a lifetime's worth of misunderstood experiences.

"But . . . " Ayano continued, taking a step toward Ibaragi's desk. "So, er, that must mean . . . Um, could you tell me your name?"

"Me? I'm Ibaragi."

"Ah, like the name of the shop. Ibaragi . . . Does that mean you, Mr. Ibaragi, and I, we're sharing the same dream?"

"Perhaps?" Ibaragi felt his heart racing like never before.

Yes, *the same dream* was such a profound turn of phrase. When it came to a partner with whom one wanted to share their whole life, it was certainly important to have *the same dream*. He could think of no better way of putting it.

"Yes, I believe so," he answered without further hesitation. A keen listener might have detected a faint tremble to his voice.

"What's come over me?" Ayano lowered her eyes.

In the corner of her vision, she caught sight of something by Ibaragi's side, involuntarily shifting her gaze.

Sensing the intensity of her stare—a rare occurrence for him—Ibaragi placed a hand on the mound of piled sixty-centimeter-wide boards. "Ah, this . . . ? It's a staircase."

"A staircase?"

"Yes. Or more precisely, a set of footboards—the parts you

stand on when you go up each step. I stumbled on them by chance, at an acquaintance's house that was due to be demolished. They were just going to be thrown away, so I took them. *These will definitely be popular,* I thought."

"Just the steps? The footboards, I mean?"

"Yes," Ibaragi said, taking one from the stack. "There are fourteen in total. I've numbered them from top to bottom, see?" He motioned to a handwritten number fourteen penciled into the corner. "This is the top one, the last step before you make it to the second floor."

"So it was a two-story house?"

Ayano found her gaze drawn to the footboards.

What kind of dream is *this?* She shook her head. But this certainly was a dreamlike turn of events. Of all things, selling the boards from a flight of stairs . . .

Before she knew it, the hour was already approaching 2:00 A.M.

Looking carefully at a clock on the far wall, she noticed that it had two second hands—without a doubt, another dream-induced fantasy. Intrigued, she tried asking the store owner about it.

"Um, that clock over there—why does it have two second hands?"

Well now! Ibaragi felt like crying out loud.

Until now, no one had ever noticed the clock's unique peculiarity. There had been those who had asked him if it was for sale, but none had remarked on its dual second hands.

His voice grew more excited as he began to explain. "That is called a *dual timepiece.* There are two separate mechanisms in the one clock."

"*Two* clocks?"

"Yes. Originally, it would lose about fifteen minutes each day, so I put another clock mechanism in to turn the second hand twice. The second mechanism tended to gain fifteen minutes each day, so I figured that by putting them together, it would be able to keep the proper time."

"I see . . . "

Ayano found it amusing that for each absurdity this dream threw at her (and this was, undeniably, a dream), she could still reflect and nod along to them all.

"So the two motors work together to keep the correct time."

She was impressed. When a positive and negative of equal magnitude met, the degree of error between them was reduced to zero. When someone facing in one direction met another facing the opposite, they achieved a perfect equilibrium. In other words, there was no need for two people to be looking the same way.

With that thought, she felt suddenly at ease.

No doubt when she woke up, she would forget all of this. Such was the nature of dreams. She might have made an important discovery here, but it would all be gone when she opened her eyes. Only this feeling of stark realization would remain in her heart, like a lingering afterimage.

I wish I didn't have to wake up, she thought.

Yes, how wonderful it would be if moments like this could occur in the waking world.

Elsewhere, on the same day, at the same time, Tashiro—a.k.a. Detective Shuro—boarded a yellow taxi, and tempted by the driver's seemingly limitless wealth of knowledge, arrived at the all-night diner Yotsukado.

No stars shone overhead.

He stood by the entrance for a long moment, listening to the taxi pull away behind him, before mustering his courage to peek through the sliding glass door at the entrance.

He spotted a group of women at the counter—one, two, three.

Three in total.

According to the driver, there were supposed to be four of them. In other words, they were one short.

Shuro, with his keen instincts, could instantly grasp what would happen next. At the same time, with a feeling of relief, he slid open the door and stepped inside like a regular customer.

"Welcome!"

Yes, there were only the three women.

Maybe she just wasn't in at this time of night, or perhaps she had the day off. In any case, he had no reason to doubt the taxi driver's information, that Ayano was the missing fourth owner.

One look at the three women standing behind the counter was enough for him to see that she wasn't there.

He took a quick glance at the menu hanging on the wall just to be sure, and had to suppress the urge to cry out in joy. Then, with a nod of his head, he called out before any of the women could come to take his order: "I'll have the ham-and-egg set."

Elsewhere, on the same day, at the same time, in a taxi painted not yellow but the color of the night sky, Matsui, after some hesitation, finally made up his mind to call the Tokyo No. 3 Consultation Room.

Despite the comical length of time he had spent debating with himself whether or not to go through with it, he didn't actually expect Kanako to be the one to pick up. After all, she had told him back in the diner that even with several operators, they still weren't able to handle the non-stop barrage of calls coming in.

As such, he reminded himself, the odds of her answering any single call were actually quite low.

But even so . . .

If he managed to get through to her, and *if* a god capable of answering one's prayers truly existed, then his wish would be to enjoy another meal with her like they had last time. Fate worked in mysterious ways—she had a habit of smiling on you whenever you managed to overcome some series of seemingly impossible obstacles.

Matsui knew full well that he might come across as a bit of a pessimist at first glance, but really he was an optimist at heart.

As such, when Kanako picked up the phone with the words "Tokyo No. 3 Consultation Room, how can I help?" Matsui was convinced that his dream was on the cusp of becoming true.

And yet—

"I'm sorry," she answered. "I have a prior engagement today."

The word *fate*, which had been swelling up in Matsui's chest to the point of suffocation, was mercilessly and unceremoniously beaten back.

He should have known. There wasn't so much as a single star out tonight.

Elsewhere, on the same day, at the same time, Mitsuki stepped through the emergency exit on the second floor of the studio prop warehouse and sat down in the middle of the stairwell to take in a lungful of fresh air.

Once more, she had felt the urge to escape to this private sanctuary. There, sitting on the landing, she noticed for the first time that the cold iron stairs of the emergency exit were painted a dark blue.

She looked up at the sky.

There were no stars. She couldn't see the moon, either. To top things off, the fire escape lights, which normally lit up the second the door was opened, were out.

It wasn't just the stairs that were blue—the stagnant air itself looked to have taken on a similar hue. She let the air wash over her, immersing herself in that ephemeral blue glow.

I wish I had a cigarette.

She had no idea how to pass the time in situations like this. Normally, she would have pulled out her cellphone, but for some reason, she wasn't quite ready to make that necessary call.

All the same, it was almost two-thirty, and Koichi would be getting ready for his early-morning newspaper run. If she dawdled, she might miss her chance, but if she called too early, he would no doubt complain about her waking him up. Five more minutes, then, she told herself. She would give him five more minutes, and then make the call.

She decided to pass the time rehearsing in her head everything that she needed to say.

There was so much she had to get across, but her feelings were still a downright mess. She was hardly proud of it, but frankly, she had never been able to give order to the chaos of her own mind.

She was always wavering between one thing and another, always so indecisive. It was only through talking things over with Koichi little by little that she had had any success organizing her thoughts. *He*, on the other hand, never said anything—or rather, the things he said never made any sense.

I've always been the one who has to make sense of whatever pops into his *mind.*

It wasn't like he listened to her problems and then offered up useful advice—it was the more that, when talking to him, she had to give her thoughts structure and meaning they otherwise lacked.

In the end, you might say that she sorted things out on her own—but she needed Koichi's silent presence to do it.

That was one of the things she had to bring up with him.

I suppose I do need someone like you after all.

But just so you know, I'm still not entirely sold on this idea of marriage. Getting married is one of the most important decisions in anyone's life. It isn't something you can make up your mind on just like that.

But fate isn't something you can decide for yourself. And you know, I've always felt like those things you don't *decide yourself tend to last the longest.*

The same goes for my current job. I joined the studio to do prop work, but before I knew it, I found myself managing the warehouse.

So you know, Koichi . . .

I also want to talk about fate. Do you remember when we first met, for that interview? You answered my questions so sincerely. It didn't have anything at all to do with the wider conversation, but I remember you saying that some people view crows as the souls of the dead.

The reason all these crows gather in Tokyo, you said, was because so many lives have been lost here.

You said they've come back, because the city is still dear to them.

Do you remember?

It's because of those words that I've followed you this far— and now I'm even considering marrying you.

Since this ring got stuck on my finger, there have been times when I tell myself that maybe I ought to just go along with it. That maybe it will all be fine.

But I don't know.

Perched on the blue steps of the emergency stairwell, Mitsuki shook her head.

And so passed her five minutes.

The old clock pointed to 1:00 A.M.

Ayano shook her head. *But it isn't really one o'clock. It has to be past that. I wonder what the real time is?*

Of course, all she had to do was pull out her cellphone if she really wanted to check.

Then again, if she was still dreaming, it didn't really matter what the time was.

According to the store owner, Ibaragi, the dual timepiece was supposed to display the correct time, but she had no way of knowing if what it showed was true in the waking world. After all, she *was* still dreaming . . .

"Um . . . "

Her best option, she decided, was to try every possibility that came to mind so that she would have no regrets when she did finally wake up.

"Are those steps for sale?"

"Yes, of course," came Ibaragi's response, a slight hint of confusion appearing between his eyebrows. "Everything here is for sale. But I haven't come up with a name for them yet."

"Then can you think of one now?"

If she had been her normal self, Ayano wouldn't have been anywhere near this forceful, but freed from her constant state of indecision, she found herself able to speak her mind.

"Once they have a name, I'll buy one."

"Really?"

Ibaragi too had cause to wonder whether he was dreaming

at this development—but in any case, he still had to assign a name to the disassembled staircase.

"Very well."

He squeezed his eyes shut for a full ten seconds, as he always did when faced with these kinds of dilemmas. In the privacy of his own thoughts, he would be able to snatch at the first words that came to mind.

"How many of them?" he murmured, not sure whether he was addressing Ayano or himself.

At last, he gave a forceful nod. "That's it. I've decided."

He opened his eyes. "For this product, each step requires a different name. They're numbered from bottom to top, with fourteen in total. So the twelfth step will be called *three-more-to-the-second-floor*. Naturally, the thirteenth one will be called *two-more-to-the-second-floor*, and the fourteenth one *one-more-to-the-second-floor*. What do you think? Which step would you like?"

Ayano closed her eyes as she too fell to thinking. Somehow, she knew that when she opened them, she would awake from the dream.

"I . . . Um . . . " She paused for a moment, but the rest flowed smoothly. "I've been climbing for so long now."

"A staircase, you mean?" Ibaragi responded, at a loss for any other reply.

"Yes . . . It's like a staircase. I've been climbing for so long, I want to go to the next floor—or the next stage of life, I suppose."

"I see . . . "

"There's a man who's been on my mind for ages now."

"Eh?" Ibaragi startled, before gently stroking the base of his thumb to soothe his tendinitis, suddenly flaring back up.

"Time passed without it leading anywhere . . . But just recently, there was a new development. I found out what he's doing now, even though I still haven't seen him in so long."

Ayano felt as if her voice belonged to someone else.

Why was she pouring her heart out to a complete stranger like this? She had never been particularly forthcoming with her private life—if anything, she had been more concerned with keeping her feelings under wraps. Though this was just a dream, she was surprised to see how strongly her emotions were welling up. Even her voice seemed to take on newfound energy.

Perhaps it was discovering the hidden strength of her desire that blew her characteristic hesitation to the wind.

"I just need one more step. One-more-to-the-second-floor. Please."

"Very well," Ibaragi said with an amiable smile, still asking himself if he wasn't caught in a dream himself.

It certainly seemed that way.

He gave himself the slightest of nods, as if to console himself.

As it turned out, he was still at the bottom of the staircase—fourteen-more-to-the-second-floor. Well, that was fine. He would have trouble selling the step furthest from the top, in any event. But no matter. He was still dreaming, and it was those dreams that made his store what it was. His was a second-hand shop, a boutique filled with miscellaneous goods that had served their original purpose—and behind it all was his dream that they might one day be of use again.

Ibaragi decided on a price of five-hundred yen for the one-more-to-the-second-floor.

"I'll take it," Ayano said, her eyes sparkling as he wrapped the footboard in a piece of blue paper.

The effort took longer than usual, on account of his injured hand, but at last he presented her with the carefully wrapped package.

Wondering why she still hadn't woken up, Ayano pulled a five-hundred-yen coin from her purse and accepted the footboard. To think that she would be able to reach the next step after all this time for just a single coin . . .

"Thank you," she said.

"No, it was my pleasure. Please come again." Ibaragi answered, staring after her as she left the store.

Once outside, Ayano held the one-more-to-the-second-floor to her chest and turned her gaze to the heavens.

Peering carefully into that deep mass of mottled black and blue, she noticed the faintest glimmer of a lone star off to the east.

Isn't the Yotsukado in that direction?

Using the star to guide her, she looked around and quickened her pace. With each step she took, reality seemed to take root within her.

Maybe this wasn't a dream after all? she realized at last.

In that case, Ichiko really had gone back to Shikoku, leaving Ayano with no other late-night refuge than the Yotsukado itself. There could be no doubt about it—this was a sign from above.

But truth be told, she didn't know the correct path through the winding alleyways between Shimokitazawa and Katatokicho to reach the diner. Her only option was to follow the star and hope that it didn't lead her astray.

Of course, she couldn't help but question herself.

What exactly am I doing?

After all, she hated walking around the city at night—was so terrified by the thought of running into trouble that she always distracted herself by calling Ichiko. But tonight there was no Ichiko. And of course, the Yotsukado was a considerable distance away, making the journey even more dangerous than usual.

But I have the stair, she reminded herself. *One-more-to-the-second-floor.*

It was only the one step, but it was still unexpectedly heavy. It wasn't so much the nighttime road as the physical weight and the distance that took a toll on her legs and back, not to mention the pervading gloom.

It wasn't just dark. They might have been painted in the same shadowy black, but there was a world of difference between a street you had passed through countless times before and a new, unfamiliar road.

The streetlights seemed to be growing fewer and farther between. Everything else around her had sunk into darkness, as if she was treading the only path that yet remained.

How long must she have walked?

Fatigue was starting to weigh down on her, and she was beginning to regret leaving the safety of her apartment—until suddenly the fog cleared, and she emerged from an alleyway onto the main street.

Even at this late hour, cars continued to stream by in either direction.

The traffic lights with their *Katatokicho* nameplates were shifting between green and red over the familiar intersection.

She arrived at the Yotsukado via a different route to the one she normally took by bicycle, which meant that the building rose up before her with an altogether different cast.

It seemed so small and precarious, but it was at the same time heartwarming to see that the store the four of them had opened all by themselves was still managing to hold on.

Ayano crossed the intersection and stood in front of the diner for a long moment. She slid the door open as quietly as possible, hoping that the others wouldn't notice. But that didn't stop Kisa and Fumina from immediately turning her way, their astonishment at her sudden appearance plain for all to see.

A moment later, Yorie, clearing up one of the tables, stared back at her with the same expression.

"Why?" the three of them asked in perfect unison.

"Today's your day off, though?"

"Did something happen?"

"Your hair's a mess."

"Well . . . " Ayano shook her head. "I don't really know how it happened. I just kind of wound up here."

"What rotten timing," Kisa exclaimed with a click of her tongue. "There was a customer asking after you. He just left, too."

"Asking after me?" Ayano leaned her blue package against the wall and tilted her head. "Who could it have been? Haruka? No, not this late at night . . . "

"It was a man. He seemed to like the ham-and-egg set. He left his business card for you. Here."

"Huh?"

The moment Ayano laid eyes on the name *Tashiro*, time seemed to stop around her. Unable to comprehend what was happening, she stood there frozen in mute silence.

"He said to tell you to call him, if you want. He seemed like a pretty good guy, right? So, who is he?"

His address and phone number were listed on the back of the card.

Maybe this is a dream after all?

He liked the ham-and-egg set?

Ayano could picture it in her mind—that small star shining high above her head.

If . . .

Kanako Fuyuki was sitting in her usual spot at her favorite bar, sipping a lemon sour the owner had whipped up for her as she attempted to put her thoughts in order.

If she hadn't finished work early tonight, she would have accepted Matsui's invitation without hesitation.

Right?

He was so gentlemanly and nice, and above all, he was happy to pick her up anywhere she needed with just one call.

Maybe I'm getting carried away . . .

It was a rare thing for someone to call her personally on the public, company line. After all, the odds that it would be her picking up were actually quite low.

It was probably an exaggeration to call this *fate*, but it was clear that some kind of mysterious connection existed between them.

Yes, if she hadn't finished early, she most definitely would have taken him up on his offer. After all, the food at that diner he liked was simply too irresistible.

Or was it because she had gone there in Matsui's company last time that it had tasted so good? Because he had so patiently lent his ear while she told him her life story?

No, it didn't really matter why.

What mattered was that it was delicious. She wanted to go there again—and again and again.

Which was why it had been so very difficult for her to say she couldn't make it today.

But she had another matter on her mind tonight . . .

"I feel kind of responsible for what happens here."

"Oh?" the woman at the bar seemed to be only half-listening. "Maybe I haven't got the full picture, but I'm not sure I'd agree. Sure, he asked you completely out of the blue, and you didn't know how to respond. But I don't know why not. It's not like I can't do this without you."

"You're sure?"

"Yes. I'm just throwing out an old phone."

She was right, of course. About a week ago, she had told Kanako she was thinking about getting rid of the pink telephone she kept in the store, seeing as no one ever used it.

"Do you know who I should contact for this kind of thing? Aren't these pink telephones supposed to be given back or something? I asked around, but no one knew what to do with it," she said, motioning to the object in question. "It was here when I took over the place, so I don't even know where it came from. It's not on a lease or anything, so I don't think it got here the usual way. I thought you might be able to help me out, since you work at that call center."

"Hmm," Kanako murmured. "Honestly, I'm still not really sure where it went, but it just so happens that we had to throw out an old phone at work recently."

"Really?"

"Yeah. A woman who runs some sort of phone funeral business came to pick it up."

"Seriously? You've gotta be kidding."

"No, that's what happened. Maybe you could ask her?"

Kanako told her about the telephone retrieval specialist Moriizumi, and the woman arranged for her to come this very night. As it happened, Kanako was due to finish up early, so she promised to stop by in advance.

But it wasn't like she needed to be there to help pick up the device.

It was certainly an overstatement to say that she was in any way responsible. All she had done was provide Moriizumi's contact information. There was no need for her to be involved beyond that. She could have simply told the woman that something had come up, that she wouldn't be able to drop by. The woman was right—it wasn't fair to turn down Matsui's invitation on account of this. No, no doubt she had simply been caught off guard by his offer, unable to commit herself.

"When was it again?" she asked, downing her lemon sour.

"Soon," the woman answered as she mixed up another glass and placed it heavily in front of Kanako.

Then, as if that was some sort of signal, there came a knock at the door.

"Excuse me," sounded a voice as Moriizumi stepped inside.

"Ah," Kanako answered with a nod and a light wave.

"Ah," Moriizumi said in turn, pointing unabashedly back at her. "The woman from the consultation room."

"You're not in mourning dress today?" Kanako looked her work clothes up and down. "Won't you have a drink?" she asked, indicating to the seat next to her.

"No. I'm on the clock." Moriizumi shook her head.

"Please."

"I said *no*."

This exchange continued for a short while, until overcome by Kanako's persistence, Moriizumi finally relented. "Just a little, then," she said, reluctantly taking the adjacent stool.

"You're drunk, aren't you, Fuyuki?" she asked without holding back.

"Huh? You remembered my name?" Kanako smiled—though as Moriizumi had pointed out, that may well have been interpreted as a sign of intoxication.

Moriizumi was quick to size up the situation. "Did you recommend me?"

"Yes, I did." Kanako, pleased that Moriizumi had remembered her name despite the fact that they hadn't exactly hit it off, was quick to reply. "Business booming?" she asked, unable to help herself.

"Not at all." Moriizumi shook her head.

The woman thoughtfully placed a non-alcoholic lemon sour, just like the one Kanako was drinking, in front of her.

Kanako promptly clinked her own glass against it. "Cheers."

Moriizumi sniffed at her own beverage as if to make sure it was non-alcoholic, glanced back at the woman, and took a hesitant sip.

This is why I hate bar pickups, she thought, but since this was the last pickup for the night, she had ultimately convinced herself that this was a convenient excuse to unwind.

"What was that?" Kanako leaned closer.

"I said business isn't booming, but I make do." Moriizumi

placed the glass back on the counter. "There's no shortage of phones that need picking up, that's for sure."

The woman behind the bar stole a sideways glance at the pink telephone on the corner of the counter. "I see."

"Ah, is that it?" Moriizumi asked, following her gaze. "They used to all be like that."

Though she looked to be at least a few years younger than Kanako and the owner, Moriizumi rested her chin on one hand and gazed at the telephone with a hint of nostalgia.

"It's funny, isn't it?" the woman said, looking back and forth at the two of them. "Your job means you're talking on the phone practically all night, while yours is all about severing phone lines."

"Ah," Kanako and Moriizumi exclaimed in perfect unison.

"I know what it feels like to want to reach out and connect with people." The woman turned to Moriizumi. "But what is it like *disconnecting* people? I suppose I should already know the answer to that one though, given my own life."

Moriizumi let out a weak chuckle "Well, everyone's different, and I never get all the details. But judging by the way people react when I pick up the telephones, some have simply moved onto a cellphone plan and don't need them anymore. Others tend to have mixed feelings. They can be very indecisive about it."

"Has anyone ever wanted to *escape*, if you know what I mean?" the bar proprietress asked, lighting a cigarette.

"Yes. Some say they want to cut off all contact with the outside world."

"So they want to sever their connections."

"I guess so. But it isn't always that simple. Some people *say* they want to make a clean break, but inside, there's someone they really do want to reach out to."

"Ah. I know the feeling."

"Yes. I had a client the other day say that. But they insisted they wouldn't be able to move on otherwise."

"Move on? Move on to what?"

"Beats me."

So that's how it is.

As Kanako listened on, the last piece of the jigsaw puzzle she had been searching for all her life seemed to click into place.

Chasing after someone you wanted to find at all costs. Someone you wanted to see, but who had decided to keep their distance for the time being. Someone you wanted to see, but decided not to. Someone you wanted to see, but couldn't.

Looking back over her own life, that desire to *meet* had taken a great many shapes and forms. Tonight too, in fact. She *did* want to see Matsui, but that honest desire was far from straightforward.

It wasn't that she *didn't* want to see him—she was simply unsure what might happen next if she went to him now.

And there's something else, she reminded herself.

Even when there was someone you desperately wanted to see, that didn't necessarily mean they felt the same way.

She and Ren had had a strong bond since early childhood, but when it came to thinking about the future, their views hadn't been perfectly aligned.

He didn't see completing puzzles—creating a unified, *finished* picture—as his next step. That had to be it.

Deep down, some part of her must have felt the same way. She was scared of completing it—afraid that, once finished, it would lose all meaning. And so she had stopped short.

The future . . . I'd kind of like to stay right here, if I can . . .

Kanako's gaze landed on the pink telephone at the end of the counter, and she found herself absentmindedly biting her lip, just as she had as a girl.

"What's that?" Kisa asked, pointing to the package propped up against the wall.

"This?" Ayano unwrapped the bundle. "I kind of bought it on impulse."

She held the piece of wood out for the others to see.

"So what *is* it?" Kisa repeated.

"A cutting board?" Fumina asked.

"It's too big for a cutting board," Yorie pointed out.

None of them could identify its true purpose.

"It's a footboard. From a flight of stairs," Ayano explained.

"Huh?" the others asked doubtfully.

"Isn't it too big?" one of them asked, but Ayano placed it down in an area with better light.

It's pretty small, actually, she thought.

If she was currently perched on this final step, she was confined to only a very small surface area. She felt like breaking down into tears at the thought that she had been stuck here for so very long—but at the same time, it felt like a perfect fit for her current situation in life.

Part of me wants to stay here just a little longer.

Nights like this aren't all that uncommon.

How many times had Matsui repeated those words to himself?

The night felt darker than usual. On such occasions, it was rare to find a great many stars glimmering over Tokyo, but tonight seemed to have gone a step further—there wasn't so much as a single star shining overhead.

It's like the end of the world . . .

Just like in that movie.

The main character had also been a taxi driver, catching some shuteye at the edge of a deserted park after an uneventful night unable to pick up any passengers. Feeling a sudden chill, Matsui snapped awake, regained his composure, and set back out to return to the job—but there still weren't any prospective customers to be found.

Only a single, dark road pressing endlessly forward.

Yes, he had practically found himself caught in the world of that film.

The only illumination came from irregular traffic lights and streetlamps. There were no other cars. Around him was a school, a cemetery, and an empty lot.

It would soon be 4:00 A.M.

At first, he thought it had to be an illusion—but no, a miniscule star had appeared in the eastern sky, as if beckoning him. Matsui decided to set off in its direction, when a muffled sound rang from his pocket.

Coming to a stop at the side of the road, he pulled out his cellphone—almost dropping it in his haste.

Looking down at the screen, the name *Kanako Fuyuki* appeared in small, flickering letters.

THE FINAL PIECE

I t was 1:00 A.M. in Tokyo.
That time came around every day. The seasons could come and go, but 1:00 A.M. was a guaranteed constant.

In the labyrinthine network of back alleys in Ginza, Eiko pushed open a door emblazoned simply with the letter *M* and peered cautiously inside. She felt so small, both mentally and physically, but she couldn't bring herself to back out now. She had heard about this place a short while back, a tiny bar comprised of little more than a counter—and while the exterior looked old and worn, the inside was brand new.

"Welcome! *Szoo.*"

Standing behind the counter was Maeda—not that Eiko could have recognized him.

As far as she was concerned, any drinking establishment would have been fine.

If Eleven Marias *is a success,* she had promised herself countless times over, *I'll go somewhere and raise a toast to my grandma. I owe it all to her.*

Now, that day had come.

Eiko was new to the city's bars and nightlife. By sheer coincidence, she had overhead a conversation between some of the promotional staff.

"Have you been to M?" one of the more senior staff members asked.

"Isn't that Maeda's place?" their younger colleague answered.

"It's pretty good. Worth checking out."

"Maybe I'll give it a look."

And so the older staff member explained how to find it.

Eiko committed the address to memory. She had more lines in the film than the other girls, and she had developed a knack for memorizing long, complicated strings of words.

"What shall I make you? *Szoo.*"

Eiko hesitated, unable to understand the menu. "Um . . . Do you have anything made with cola?" she asked. If at all possible, she wanted to celebrate her grandmother with the same drink she requested at the very end.

"Of course."

Maeda had taken Mitsuki's comments in the prop warehouse to heart.

Not only did he remember them verbatim—they had pushed him to make the decision to return to bartending.

It helped that another bar was closing down right around the same time and that, to his surprise, the studio had offered its financial support. By far the most significant factor, however, was Mitsuki's remark that there was something romantic about an experienced silver fox preparing drinks, and her insistence that she would frequent a place like that almost every day.

"How about a Whiskey and Coke? *Szoo.*"

As fortune would have it, that was the very drink he had prepared for Mitsuki on the night of the earthquake.

"Yes, I'll try that."

Eiko had no idea what a Whiskey and Coke was. After all, she had just turned drinking age, so visiting a bar was a new experience for her.

As late as it was, there were no other patrons. She had the whole bar to herself. It was practically a private booking.

If it were me, I'd go there every day.

With those words reverberating in his chest, Maeda prepared the young woman's order.

He had often walked with a hunched back during his time

as a warehouse manager, but curiously, the moment he put on a bowtie and stepped behind the bar again, he felt his posture straightening as it had when he was a young man. How had he let himself get so lost?

The Whiskey and Coke was bitingly cold. He had always been particular about preparing drinks as cold as possible, but this time, when he poured it out into a glass and sat it down on the countertop, the carbonation and the cold air combined to form a fine mist around the glass.

"Here you go," he said, his voice barely audible.

Eiko lowered her hand from her chest to take the glass—withdrawing it at once after being struck by its frigid temperature.

The amber-colored drink, so dark it was almost black, was garnished with a crescent-shaped slice of lemon.

Lured by its enticing aroma, she took hold of it once more and raised it to her lips.

From the first sip, she felt not that she was consuming alcohol, but rather as if her mouth was filled with the essence of the quiet late-night solitude of the bar itself.

An inexplicable sense of joy at discovering this new side of nighttime Tokyo seeped into her throat.

"It's delicious," she murmured.

Around the same time, Mitsuki and Koichi were enjoying a meal at the counter of the Yotsukado in Katatokicho. For Mitsuki, this was only her second time visiting the diner, while for Koichi, it was his first.

"It's nice, this place, right?" Mitsuki asked, acting as though she were a regular customer, watching the women hard at work behind the counter. For some reason, just being close to them had a soothing effect on her mental state. *Ah, I am alive,* she wanted to say from the bottom of her heart.

"Matsui told me about this place," she explained.

"Ah . . . the taxi driver?" Koichi answered, scrambling to recall where he had heard her mention that name before.

"Yes. Matsui, from Blackbird. The all-night taxi company. I can't tell you how much he's helped me over the years. But he didn't tell me about this diner until just recently. I can't forgive him for keeping it a secret so long. And what's worse, he had no problem sharing it with Kanako, but he kept me in the dark."

"She was here yesterday," Ayano called out from behind the counter. "They both were. They're getting very close."

"Kanako?" Koichi tried to locate the name in his memories, to little success.

"You know, from back then . . . " Mitsuki began, placing her half-eaten piece of karaage chicken back on her plate. "The loquat thief."

"Ah. That was Kanako?" Koichi nodded in understanding.

"Loquat thief?" Ayano repeated. "What do you mean?"

"It's a long story," Mitsuki said, munching on a piece of chicken. "Anyway, that's how the two of them first met. There's a bit of an age gap between them, but they seem to have hit it off well."

"Because of that loquat thief incident?"

"Actually, I think it was more that they've both been looking for someone. Right?" Mitsuki gave Ayano a meaningful look. "Like I said, it's a long story. Completely by chance, he picked up a famous detective, you see?" She paused to gauge Ayano's reaction. "They were thinking of hiring him, the both of them . . . Speaking of which, what happened with that?"

Ayano wiped her hands with a kitchen rag. "Well . . . " she began in a small voice.

"No." Shuro was quick to shake his head. "I haven't taken on any jobs from Matsui or Kanako."

"You haven't?" Ayano answered from across the counter, struck by a sense of wonder at the chain of events that had brought them both here.

It's like something from a fairytale.

Lately, Shuro had become a regular at the Yotsukado, always ordering the ham-and-egg set. Ayano had given up on ever seeing him again, and so was endlessly grateful to Matsui and Kanako for having made this reunion possible. But at the same time, she couldn't help but wonder what had happened to those people they were both looking for.

"As far as I know, Matsui was looking for a woman, a passenger he picked up a long time ago. It was love at first sight, apparently. He's never told us about it in full, but I think she reminded him of an ex-girlfriend or something like that. I heard him tell Kanako he'd like to see her again one day, if at all possible."

"I see." Having finished his meal, Shuro poured himself a glass of hot hojicha tea.

"And Kanako, she's looking for her younger brother. He ran away from home about twelve years ago, I think. She wanted to see him again, too. So that's how the two of them bonded, over their desire to find people who had left their lives."

"I see," Shuro repeated, nodding as he sipped his tea. "So that's it. Their feelings must have changed when they realized they had common ground."

"Changed?"

"Yeah. It's pretty simple, really. Especially in Matsui's case. After meeting Kanako, he's realized he doesn't need to find that phantom woman anymore."

"Ah. I see what you mean."

"And as for Kanako . . . To tell you the truth, I have an idea where she might look for her brother . . . "

"Eh?"

"I might know where he is."

"You do?"

"Well, I won't be able to say for sure until I hear the details directly from her. I've only met her twice in passing, here at the Yotsukado. She told me about her job, and I mentioned my detective work. I told her to reach out if she ever needed help with anything."

"That's our resident detective for you!" Kisa, who had been eavesdropping from further down the counter, suddenly exclaimed. "He's already figured out what's been bothering her!"

"No, it isn't like that," Shuro insisted. "I just happen to overhear people talking, and I put all the pieces together like with a jigsaw puzzle. That's all there is to it. She mentioned her brother running away from home more than a decade ago . . . "

"Do you know her brother?"

"Maybe. I realized just now I might have been carrying the last piece of the puzzle here in my pocket all along."

Shuro's reputation as a great detective was due, in part, to his exceptional sense of intuition.

He would be the first to admit that his intuition wasn't attributable to any special abilities, but rather was simply about realizing how one thing connected to another.

Almost a year had passed since he had traveled to the outskirts of Tokyo to watch a movie in which his father featured, meeting there a young man—technically, a thirty-six-year-old man who came across as young in the dark of night—by the name of Ren Fuyuki. In Shuro's mind, he overlapped perfectly with Kanako's missing younger brother.

I'd like to see him again.

It wasn't Matsui or Kanako who murmured this, but rather the detective.

The reason was simple—nearly a year on, Shuro had learned that the movie theater would soon be screening a double feature of two extremely minor films in which his father had appeared. Naturally, he wanted to see the movies—but he also wanted to ask Ren if he was behind this project. After all, he was just a part-time worker.

When Shuro stopped by the cinema, however, he was

surprised to learn that Ren had been promoted from a part-timer all the way to manager. Faced with an ever-dwindling turnout of moviegoers, the previous manager, it just so happened, had thrown in the towel—and Ren's approach of structuring programming around the films that he himself wanted to watch had led to an unexpected rebound.

"So that's how the double feature came about."

Shuro felt encouraged to find that Ren had slipped easily into the role of curator, even if it meant he wouldn't be trying his hand as a detective any time soon.

"To tell you the truth, I didn't come here just to see my father's films," he admitted. "There's something else I wanted to ask you—about the sister you mentioned last time."

"My sister?" Ren asked.

"Yes. Her name's Kanako, isn't it?"

"It is . . . What about her?"

"Does she have a dimple on her right cheek when she smiles?"

"Yes. She was born with it."

"So I was right. She's currently working as an operator at the Tokyo No. 3 Consultation Room, helping people with all kinds of problems."

"Oh?"

"But there's a personal matter she's never been able share with anyone—that she wants to see her brother again after he disappeared nearly thirteen years ago."

"Me, you mean?"

"Yes. Or rather, she did. I don't know if it's the distance of time that's driving this or if she's had a change of heart, but recently, I think she may have given up on finding you. This is just speculation on my part, but I think she's figured it out—what you told me about her smothering you with kindness."

"She has?"

"I think so, yes."

"Really?"

Ren remained silent for a long moment, before finally murmuring: "I don't know what to say. I mean, I'm glad to hear that. But it's also kind of sad . . . " He squeezed his eyes shut. "I don't really know how to describe it," he said with a shake of his head.

After hearing Shuro's story from Ayano, Koichi set his chopsticks down with a weak sigh. "So Kanako has no idea that her brother is managing a movie theater now?"

"It sounds like it," Ayano admitted.

In a one-room apartment roughly eight kilometers to the northeast, Kanako let out a sudden sneeze.

This was enough to remind her of a caller she had the other day: "I can't stop sneezing. It has to mean someone's talking about me behind my back, right?"

"Are you sure you haven't just caught a cold?" she asked—but now she found herself in the same boat, and she too almost wanted to call someone for advice.

She stared at her reflection in the mirror.

Tonight's the night, she told herself.

She had the day off work, and the weather was perfect—the night sky overcast, and the moon hidden. She reverently pulled on the black raincoat that she had just gotten back from the dry cleaners and added a black hat slung low over her eyes.

A full year had passed.

The hem of her coat fluttering, Kanako stepped briskly out from the room.

A full year. That was how long she had known Matsui.

Is it that long already? The older I get, the quicker time seems to fly by. Does that mean I've been doing this loquat thief thing for thirteen years now? Maybe it's time to call it quits. Climbing trees is starting to get more difficult than it used to be . . .

She headed straight for the nearest bus route.

The night was lonely, with neither stars nor moon in the sky overhead, but she wasn't about to let that diminish her determination. Her heart pounding, she made her way over the pedestrian crossing.

In the light of the streetlamps, she came across a loquat tree.

"Alright," sounded her hushed voice.

It didn't take long for her to spot the orange fruit.

Plants were amazing things. Every year, without fail, they created literal, solid produce.

But just before she could ready herself for the climb, those beads of orange were suddenly obscured by a murky darkness.

Huh?

Some black mass—probably a crow—looked to have snatched one of the fruits.

No, hold on. She had never seen a crow *that* big before.

"Hello?" she called out.

The next moment, a voice sounded back: "Eh?" A man's voice—one she couldn't possibly forget.

"Who's there?" she asked, peering into the branches.

"I'm a loquat thief," came the unmistakable voice of her younger brother.

Mitsuki was yet to learn that all this was taking place a mere eight kilometers from the diner.

Eventually, word would reach her on a future visit, and she would wonder at the chain of events that had made it all possible—but that was still a long way off.

Whenever Mitsuki heard a story like that, she couldn't help but break into a weak smile and think to herself that everyone else was moving forward with their lives while she remained the same as ever.

Nothing changed. She didn't even try to change. She just kept on letting every opportunity that life threw at her fly past . . .

For her, the phrase *the same as ever* had two meanings. The first was an expression of relief and satisfaction that events hadn't taken a turn for the worse. The second was as a sign of self-deprecation, a means of mocking herself for remaining ever predictable, for never venturing forth from the fixed, rigid outlines of the life she had built.

"Thanks," she said to the women as she and Koichi left the diner.

Outside, the two stood in silence, staring up at the empty night sky.

They remained that way for a short while, until Koichi finally broke the silence. "Where to now?" He stood at the edge of the intersection, eyes squeezed tightly shut as if reading the course of the wind.

"Anywhere is fine," Mitsuki answered softly.

Koichi must have noticed the weakness in her voice, as all at once, he started bellowing out some strange song.

"What is that? That song?"

She was sure she had never heard that nonsensical tune before, with its unfamiliar lyrics and melody, when she suddenly realized something.

Is this the first time I've heard Koichi sing?

"Good morning, Tokyo—it's almost sunrise," he sang at the top of this voice. Or at least, that was what she thought he was saying.

"What's the name of the song?"

"I sometimes sing this when I'm out delivering the morning papers."

"I asked you what it's called," she said again.

Koichi, however, kept on singing, until eventually, Mitsuki found herself joining in.

Before she knew it, they were *both* singing at the top of their voices.

And as they sang, they began to walk, without any particular destination in mind.

"Good morning, Tokyo—it's almost sunrise."

But morning eventually gives way to day, and day to night, the pale moonlight falling once more over Tokyo's diners, its bars, its antiques shops, its film studios, and its telephone consultation rooms.

And of course, Matsui's midnight-blue taxi was once again out on the streets.

"I can't *do* this," Mitsuki moaned, much the same as she always did. "There's no way I can find a pair of sheep shears in the middle of the night."

"It's too early to give up," Matsui consoled her.

"No, this time it really *is* impossible," Mitsuki insisted.

"Let's keep looking a little longer," Matsui suggested. "We've managed to find everything you've needed this far, haven't we? Right, let's try that odd antiques store again . . . "

Matsui checked on Mitsuki in the rearview mirror. She was still fiddling with the silver ring on her left ring finger, still as stuck as the day she first put it on. Perhaps she wasn't even aware of her fingertips slowly tracing its glossy surface.

At that moment, she let out a weak sigh—or so it seemed. Her face had taken on a complicated look, a puzzling mix of confusion and shock.

She was staring at her own hands.

After checking the road ahead of him, he peered more deeply into the mirror.

"It might be coming loose," Mitsuki murmured—when just like that, the silver ring slipped all the way to her fingertip, almost falling right off. Its surface gleamed faintly in the light of passing streetlamps.

"Ah," she breathed softly. "It came off."

After the briefest of pauses, she hurriedly put it back in place.

There's a certain style of writing known as the serial short story—a collection of short stories that at first glance appear to be separate tales, but which are actually connected to one another, and which can in fact be read as a full-length novel.

Goodnight Tokyo is one such collection of serial short stories—but my intention could perhaps be better described as a collection of *intersecting* short stories.

Intersections are of particular importance in this work. To begin with, we have a prominent crossroads, where we find a diner run by four women. We might as well name their narrative arc after the establishment that serves as its backdrop, so *Yotsukado* it is.

Then we have a man named Matsui, a taxi driver who, like the diner, operates only at night. He has dreamed of becoming a cab driver ever since reading a children's story by Kimiko Aman when he was a kid, *The Car Is the Color of the Sky*. Come to think of it, *The Car Is the Color of the Sky* is another collection of serial short stories, and the main character has the exact same name as our own Matsui. But since *our* Matsui only works at night, we should perhaps call his arc *The Car Is the Color of the Night Sky*.

One of this night taxi's regular customers is a woman named Mitsuki, whose job entails finding props for the film company where she works. We might title the next arc *Mitsuki the Procurer*, in which, while attempting to source loquats in the middle of the night, she meets a certain woman.

This woman, in turn, works at the Tokyo No. 3 Consultation Room, a jack-of-all-trades telephone consultation service—and to her arc we might give the title *Voices in the Night*.

Then comes *The Veranda Bat*, following another woman, Moriizumi, who goes about collecting unused telephones—leading to an encounter with our call center operator.

On top of this, we have *Detective Shuro and the Twenty Keys*, which describes the adventures of a strange private detective who hops into Matsui's cab one fateful night.

Until We Become Mary follows the struggles of eleven young actresses set to appear in an upcoming movie, *The Last Piece of the Jigsaw* features a man in the sunset years of youth, working to rebuild a crumbling movie theater, and we also have *Tokyo Whiskey and Coke*, about the recollections of a late-middle-aged man opening a small bar in a Ginza back alley.

Oh, and there's one more—*Ibaragi and the Two Moons*, following the humorous daily life of a secondhand shop owner in Shimokitazawa.

That's ten books.

No, excuse me. Those ten books exist only in my mind, at least for the time being.

But the novel *Goodnight Tokyo* is the result of the intersection of these ten fantastic tales.

It is, I hope, a collection of serial short stories that can be enjoyed as ten books in one.

August 2018

Born in Tokyo in 1962, Atsuhiro Yoshida is an award-winning book designer and renowned author of over forty books. Already published in French, German, and Italian, *Goodnight Tokyo* is Yoshida's English-language debut.